Cimorene left in disgust and went out to the castle garden. She was very discouraged. It looked as if she were going to marry the prince of Sathem-by-the-Mountains whether she wanted to or not.

"I'd rather be eaten by a dragon," she muttered.

"That can be arranged," said a voice from beside her left slipper.

Cimorene looked down and saw a small green frog looking up at her. "I beg your pardon. Did you speak?" she asked.

"You don't see anyone else around, do you?" said the frog.

"Oh!" said Cimorene. She had never met a talking frog before. "Are you an enchanted prince?" she asked a little doubtfully.

"No, but I've met a couple of them, and after a while you pick up a few things," said the frog. "Now, why is it that you want to be eaten by a dragon?"

Also in the Point Fantasy series:

POINT FANTASY

DRAGONSBANE

The Enchanted Forest Chronicles

BOOK ONE

Patricia C. Wrede

Cover illustration by Paul Young

■SCHOLASTIC

*For Alan Carl and Annie Bujold, because
they liked the other one a lot*

Scholastic Children's Books,
Scholastic Publications Ltd,
7–9 Pratt Street, London NW1 0AE, UK

Scholastic Inc.,
730 Broadway, New York, NY 10003, USA

Scholastic Canada Ltd,
123 Newkirk Road, Richmond Hill,
Ontario, Canada L4C 3G5

Ashton Scholastic Pty Ltd,
P O Box 579, Gosford, New South Wales,
Australia

Ashton Scholastic Ltd,
Private Bag 1, Penrose, Auckland,
New Zealand

First published in the USA by Harcourt Brace & Company, 1990
This edition first published by Scholastic Inc., 1992
First published in the UK by Scholastic Publications Ltd, 1993

Text copyright © Patricia C. Wrede, 1990
Cover illustration copyright © Paul Young, 1993

ISBN 0 590 55292 9

Typeset by Quadraset Ltd, Midsomer Norton, Avon
Printed by Cox & Wyman Ltd, Reading, Berks

10 9 8 7 6 5 4 3 2 1

CONTENTS

CHAPTER 1

In Which Cimorene Refuses to Be Proper and Has a Conversation with a Frog

Linderwall was a large kingdom, just east of the Mountains of Morning, where philosophers were highly respected and the number five was fashionable. The climate was unremarkable. The knights kept their armor brightly polished mainly for show — it had been centuries since a dragon had come east. There were the usual periodic problems with royal children and uninvited fairy godmothers, but they were always the sort of thing that could be cleared up by finding the proper prince or princess to marry the unfortunate child a few years later. All in all, Linderwall was a very prosperous and pleasant place.

Cimorene hated it.

Cimorene was the youngest daughter of the King of Linderwall, and her parents found her rather trying. Their first six daughters were perfectly normal princesses, with long, golden hair and sweet dispositions, each more beautiful than the last. Cimorene was lovely enough, but her hair was jet black, and she wore it in braids instead of curled and pinned like her sisters.

And she wouldn't stop growing. Her parents were quite sure that no prince would want to marry a girl who could look him in the eye instead of gazing up at him becomingly through her lashes. As for the girl's disposition – well, when people were being polite, they said she was strong-minded. When they were angry or annoyed with her, they said she was as stubborn as a pig.

The King and Queen did the best they could. They hired the most superior tutors and governesses to teach Cimorene all the things a princess ought to know – dancing, embroidery, drawing, and etiquette. There was a great deal of etiquette, from the proper way to curtsy before a visiting prince to how loudly it was permissible to scream when being carried off by a giant. (Linderwall still had an occasional problem with giants.)

Cimorene found it all very dull, but she pressed her lips together and learned it anyway. When she couldn't stand it any longer, she would go down to the castle armory and bully the armsmaster into giving her a fencing lesson. As she got older, she found her regular lessons more and more boring. Consequently, the fencing lessons became more and more frequent.

When she was twelve, her father found out.

"Fencing is not proper behavior for a princess," he told her in the gentle-but-firm tone recommended by the court philosopher.

Cimorene tilted her head to one side. "Why not?"

"It's . . . well, it's simply not done."

Cimorene considered. "Aren't I a princess?"

"Yes, of course you are, my dear," said her father with relief. He had been bracing himself for a storm of tears, which was the way his other daughters reacted to reprimands.

"Well, I fence," Cimorene said with the air of one delivering an unshakable argument. "So it is *too* done by a princess."

"That doesn't make it proper, dear," put in her mother gently.

"Why not?"

"It simply doesn't," the Queen said firmly, and that was the end of Cimorene's fencing lessons.

3

When she was fourteen, her father discovered that she was making the court magician teach her magic.

"How long has this been going on?" he asked wearily when she arrived in response to his summons.

"Since you stopped my fencing lessons," Cimorene said. "I suppose you're going to tell me it isn't proper behavior for a princess."

"Well, yes. I mean, it isn't proper."

"Nothing interesting seems to be proper," Cimorene said.

"You might find things more interesting if you applied yourself a little more, dear," Cimorene's mother said.

"I doubt it," Cimorene muttered, but she knew better than to argue when her mother used that tone of voice. And that was the end of the magic lessons.

The same thing happened over the Latin lessons from the court philosopher, the cooking lessons from the castle chef, the economics lessons from the court treasurer, and the juggling lessons from the court minstrel. Cimorene began to grow rather tired of the whole business.

When she was sixteen, Cimorene summoned her fairy godmother.

"Cimorene, my dear, this sort of thing really

isn't done," the fairy said, fanning away the scented blue smoke that had accompanied her appearance.

"People keep telling me that," Cimorene said.

"You should pay attention to them, then," her godmother said irritably. "I'm not used to being hauled away from my tea without warning. And you aren't supposed to call me unless it is a matter of utmost importance to your life and future happiness."

"It *is* of utmost importance to my life and future happiness," Cimorene said.

"Oh, very well. You're a bit young to have fallen in love already; still, you always have been a precocious child. Tell me about him."

Cimorene sighed. "It isn't a him."

"Enchanted, is he?" the fairy said with a spark of interest. "A frog, perhaps? That used to be quite popular, but it seems to have gone out of fashion lately. Nowadays, all the princes are talking birds, or dogs, or hedgehogs."

"No, no, I'm not in love with anyone!"

"Then what, exactly, is your problem?" the fairy said in exasperation.

"This!" Cimorene gestured at the castle around her. "Embroidery lessons, and dancing, and – and being a princess!"

"My dear Cimorene!" the fairy said, shocked. "It's your heritage!"

"It's boring."

"Boring?" The fairy did not appear to believe what she was hearing.

"Boring. I want to do things, not sit around all day and listen to the court minstrel make up songs about how brave Daddy is and how lovely his wife and daughters are."

"Nonsense, my dear. This is just a stage you're going through. You'll outgrow it soon, and you'll be very glad you didn't do anything rash."

Cimorene looked at her godmother suspiciously. "You've been talking to my parents, haven't you?"

"Well, they do try to keep me up to date on what my godchildren are doing."

"I thought so," said Cimorene, and bade her fairy godmother a polite goodbye.

A few weeks later, Cimorene's parents took her to a tourney in Sathem-by-the-Mountains, the next kingdom over. Cimorene was quite sure that they were only taking her because her fairy godmother had told them that something had better be done about her, and soon. She kept this opinion to herself. Anything was better than the endless rounds of dancing and embroidery lessons at home.

Cimorene realized her mistake almost as soon

as they reached their destination, for the King of Sathem-by-the-Mountains had a son. He was a golden-haired, blue-eyed, and exceedingly handsome prince, whose duties appeared to consist entirely of dancing attendance on Cimorene.

"*Isn't* he handsome!" Cimorene's lady-in-waiting sighed.

"Yes," Cimorene said without enthusiasm. "Unfortunately, he isn't anything else."

"Whatever do you mean?" the lady-in-waiting said in astonishment.

"He has no sense of humor, he isn't intelligent, he can't talk about anything except tourneys, and half of what he does say he gets wrong. I'm glad we're only staying three weeks. I don't think I could stand to be polite to him for much longer than that."

"But what about your engagement?" the lady-in-waiting cried, horrified.

"What engagement?" Cimorene said sharply.

The lady-in-waiting tried to mutter something about a mistake, but Cimorene put up her chin in her best princess fashion and insisted on an explanation. Finally, the lady-in-waiting broke down.

"I . . . I overheard Their Majesties discussing it yesterday." She sniffled into her handkerchief. "The stipulations and convenants and contracts and settlements have all been drawn up, and they're going to sign them the day after to-morrow and announce it on Th-Thursday."

"I see," said Cimorene. "Thank you for telling me. You may go."

The lady-in-waiting left, and Cimorene went to see her parents. They were annoyed and embarrassed to find that Cimorene had discovered their plans, but they were still very firm about it. "We were going to tell you tomorrow, when we signed the papers," her father said.

"We knew you'd be pleased, dear," her mother said, nodding. "He's *such* a good-looking boy."

"But I don't want to marry Prince Therandil," Cimorene said.

"Well, it's not exactly a brilliant match," Cimorene's father said, frowning. "But I didn't think you'd care how big his kingdom is."

"It's the prince I don't care for," Cimorene said.

"That's a great pity, dear, but it can't be helped," Cimorene's mother said placidly. "I'm afraid it isn't likely that you'll get another offer."

"Then I won't get married at all."

Both her parents looked slightly shocked. "My dear Cimorene!" said her father. "That's out of the question. You're a princess; it simply isn't *done*."

"I'm too young to get married!"

"Your Great-Aunt Rose was married at sixteen," her mother pointed out. "One really can't count all those years she spent asleep under that dreadful fairy's curse."

"I won't marry the prince of Sathem-by-the-Mountains!" Cimorene said desperately. "It isn't proper!"

"What?" said both her parents together.

"He hasn't rescued me from a giant or an ogre or freed me from a magic spell," Cimorene said.

Both her parents looked uncomfortable. "Well, no," said Cimorene's father. "It's a bit late to start arranging it, but we might be able to manage something."

"I don't think it's necessary," Cimorene's mother said. She looked reprovingly at Cimorene. "You've never paid attention to what was or wasn't suitable before, dear; you can't start now. Proper or not, you will marry Prince Therandil three weeks from Thursday."

"But, Mother—"

"I'll send the wardrobe mistress to your room to start fitting your bride clothes," Cimorene's mother said firmly, and that was the end of the conversation.

Cimorene decided to try a more direct approach. She went to see Prince Therandil. He was in the castle armory, looking at swords. "Good morning, Princess," he said when he finally noticed Cimorene. "Don't you think this is a lovely sword?"

Cimorene picked it up. "The balance is off."

"I believe you're right," said Therandil after a moment's study. "Pity; now I'll have to find another. Is there something I can do for you?"

"Yes," said Cimorene. "You can *not* marry me."

"What?" Therandil looked confused.

"You don't really want to marry me, do you?" Cimorene said coaxingly.

"Well, not exactly," Therandil replied. "I mean, in a way. That is—"

"Oh, good," Cimorene said, correctly interpreting this muddled reply as *No, not at all*. "Then you'll tell your father you don't want to marry me?"

"I couldn't do that!" Therandil said, shocked. "It wouldn't be right."

"Why not?" Cimorene demanded crossly.

"Because – because – well, because princes just don't do that!"

"Then how are you going to keep from marrying me?"

"I guess I won't be able to," Therandil said after thinking hard for a moment. "How do you like that sword over there? The one with the silver hilt?"

Cimorene left in disgust and went out to

the castle garden. She was very discouraged. It looked as if she were going to marry the prince of Sathem-by-the-Mountains whether she wanted to or not.

"I'd rather be eaten by a dragon," she muttered.

"That can be arranged," said a voice from beside her left slipper.

Cimorene looked down and saw a small green frog looking up at her. "I beg your pardon. Did you speak?" she asked.

"You don't see anyone else around, do you?" said the frog.

"Oh!" said Cimorene. She had never met a talking frog before. "Are you an enchanted prince?" she asked a little doubtfully.

"No, but I've met a couple of them, and after a while you pick up a few things," said the frog. "Now, why is it that you want to be eaten by a dragon?"

"My parents want me to marry Prince Therandil," Cimorene explained.

"And you don't want to? Sensible of you," said the frog. "I don't like Therandil. He used to skip rocks across the top of my pond. They always sank into my living room."

"I'm sorry," Cimorene said politely.

"Well," said the frog, "what are you going to do about it?"

"Marrying Therandil? I don't know. I've tried

talking to my parents, but they won't listen, and neither will Therandil."

"I didn't ask what you'd *said* about it," the frog snapped. "I asked what you're going to do. Nine times out of ten, talking is a way of avoiding doing things."

"What kind of things would you suggest?" Cimorene said, stung.

"You could challenge the prince to a duel," the frog suggested.

"He'd win," Cimorene said. "It's been four years since I've been allowed to do any fencing."

"You could turn him into a toad."

"I never got past invisibility in my magic lessons," Cimorene said. "Transformations are advanced study."

The frog looked at her disapprovingly. "Can't you do anything?"

"I can curtsy," Cimorene said disgustedly. "I know seventeen different country dances, nine ways to agree with an ambassador from Cathay without actually promising him anything, and one hundred and forty-three embroidery stitches. And I can make cherries jubilee."

"Cherries jubilee?" asked the frog, and snapped at a passing fly.

"The castle chef taught me, before Father made him stop," Cimorene explained.

The frog munched briefly, then swallowed

and said, "I suppose there's no help for it. You'll have to run away."

"Run away?" Cimorene said. "I don't like that idea. Too many things could go wrong."

"You don't like the idea of marrying Prince Therandil, either," the frog pointed out.

"Maybe I can think of some other way out of getting married."

The frog snorted. "Such as?" Cimorene didn't answer, and after a moment the frog said, "I thought so. Do you want my advice or not?"

"Yes, please," said Cimorene. After all, she didn't have to follow it.

"Go to the main road outside the city and follow it away from the mountains," said the frog. "After a while, you will come to a small pavilion made of gold, surrounded by trees made of silver with emerald leaves. Go straight past it without stopping, and don't answer if anyone calls out to you from the pavilion. Keep on until you reach a hovel. Walk straight up to the door and knock three times, then snap your fingers and go inside. You'll find some people there who can help you out of your difficulties if you're polite about asking and they're in the right mood. And that's all."

The frog turned abruptly and dived into the pool. "Thank you very much," Cimorene called after it, thinking that the frog's advice sounded very odd indeed. She rose and went back into the castle.

She spent the rest of the day being fitted and fussed over by her ladies-in-waiting until she was ready to scream. By the end of the formal banquet, at which she had to sit next to Prince Therandil and listen to endless stories of his prowess in battle, Cimorene was more than ready to take the frog's advice.

Late that night, when most of the castle was asleep, Cimorene bundled up five clean handkerchiefs and her best crown. Then she dug out the notes she had taken during her magic lessons and carefully cast a spell of invisibility. It seemed to work, but she was still very watchful as she sneaked out of the castle. After all, it had been a long time since she had practised.

By morning, Cimorene was well outside the city and visible again, walking down the main road that led away from the mountains. It was hot and dusty, and she began to wish she had brought a bottle of water instead of the handkerchiefs.

Just before noon, she spied a small grove of trees next to the road ahead of her. It looked like a cool, pleasant place to rest for a few minutes, and she hurried forward. When she reached the grove, however, she saw that the trees were made of the finest silver, and their shining green leaves were huge emeralds. In the center of the grove stood a charming pavilion made of gold and hung with gold curtains.

Cimorene slowed down and looked longingly at the cool green shade beneath the trees. Just then a woman's voice called out, "My dear, you look so tired and thirsty! Come and sit with me and share my luncheon."

The voice was so kind and coaxing that Cimorene took two steps towards the edge of the road before she remembered the frog's advice. *Oh, no,* she thought to herself, *I'm not going to be caught this easily!* She turned without saying anything and hurried on down the road.

A little farther on she came to a tiny, wretched-looking hovel made of cracked and weathered gray boards. The door hung slant-wise on a broken hinge, and the whole building looked as though it were going to topple over at any moment. Cimorene stopped and stared doubtfully at it, but she had followed the frog's advice this far, and she thought it would be silly to stop now. So she shook the dust from her skirts and put on her crown (so as to make a good impression). She marched up to the door, knocked three times, and snapped her fingers just as the frog had told her. Then she pushed the door open and went in.

CHAPTER 2

In Which Cimorene Discovers the Value of a Classical Education and Has Some Unwelcome Visitors

Inside, the hovel was dark and cool and damp. Cimorene found it a pleasant relief after the hot, dusty road, but she wondered why no sunlight seemed to be coming through the cracks in the boards. She was still standing just inside the door, waiting for her eyes to adjust to the dark, when someone said crossly, "Is this that princess we've been waiting for?"

"Why don't you ask her?" said a deep voice.

"I'm Princess Cimorene of Linderwall," Cimorene answered politely. "I was told you could help me."

"Help her?" said the first voice, and Cimorene heard a snort. "I think we should just eat her and be done with it."

Cimorene felt frightened. She wondered if the voices belonged to ogres or trolls and if she could slip out of the hovel before they made up their minds about eating her. She felt behind her for the door and started in surprise when her fingers touched damp stone instead of dry wood. Then a third voice said, "Not so fast, Woraug. Let's hear her story first."

So Cimorene took a deep breath and began to explain about the fencing lessons and the magic lessons, and the Latin and the juggling, and all the other things that weren't considered proper behavior for a princess, and she told the voices that she had run away from Sathem-by-the-Mountains to keep from having to marry Prince Therandil.

"And what do you expect us to do about it?" one of the voices asked curiously.

"I don't know," Cimorene said. "Except, of course, that I *would* rather not be eaten. I can't see who you are in this dark, you know."

"That can be fixed," said the voice. A moment later, a small ball of light appeared in the air above Cimorene's head. Cimorene stepped backward very quickly and ran into the wall.

The voices belonged to dragons.

Five of them lay on, sprawled over or curled around the various rocks and columns that filled the huge cave where Cimorene stood. Each of the males (there were three) had two short, stubby, sharp-looking horns on either side of their heads; the female dragon had three, one on each side and one in the center of her forehead. The last dragon was still too young to have made up its mind which sex it wanted to be; it didn't have any horns at all.

Cimorene felt very frightened. The smallest of the dragons was easily three times as tall as she was, and they gave an overwhelming impression of shining green scales and sharp silver teeth. They were much scarier in person than in the pictures she remembered from her natural history books. She swallowed very hard, wondering whether she really *would* rather be eaten by a dragon than marry Therandil.

"Well?" said the three-horned dragon just in front of her. "Just what are you asking us to do for you?"

"I—" Cimorene stopped short as an idea occurred to her. Cautiously, she asked, "Dragons are . . . are fond of princesses, aren't they?"

"Very," said the dragon, and smiled. The smile showed all her teeth, which Cimorene did not find reassuring.

"That is, I've heard of dragons who have captive princesses to cook for them and – and so on," said Cimorene, who had very little idea what captive princesses did all day.

The dragon in front of Cimorene nodded. One of the others, a yellowish green in color, shifted restlessly and said, "Oh, let's just go ahead and eat her. It will save trouble."

Before any of the other dragons could answer, there was a loud, booming noise, and a sixth dragon slithered into the cave. His scales were more gray than green, and the dragons by the door made way for him respectfully.

"Kazul!" said the newcomer in a loud voice. "*Achoo!* Sorry I'm late, but a terrible thing happened on the way here, *achoo!*"

"What was it?" said the dragon to whom Cimorene had been talking.

"Ran into a wizard. *Achoo!* Had to eat him; no help for it. *Achoo, achoo.* And now look at me!" Every time the gray-green dragon sneezed, he emitted a small ball of fire that scorched the wall of the cave.

"Calm down, Roxim," said Kazul. "You're only making it worse."

"*Achoo!* Calm down? When I'm having an allergy attack? *Achoo*, oh bother, *achoo!*" said the gray-green dragon. "Somebody give me a handkerchief. *Achoo!*"

"Here," said Cimorene, holding out one of the ones she had brought with her. "Use this." She was beginning to feel much less frightened, for the gray-green dragon reminded her of her great-uncle, who was old and rather hard of hearing and of whom she was rather fond.

"What's that?" said Roxim. *Achoo!* Oh, hurry up and give it here."

Kazul took the handkerchief from Cimorene, using two claws very delicately, and passed it to Roxim. The gray-green dragon mopped his streaming eyes and blew his nose. "That's better, I think. *Achoo!* Oh, drat!"

The ball of fire that accompanied the dragon's sneeze had reduced the handkerchief to a charred scrap. Cimorene hastily dug out another one and handed it to Kazul, feeling very glad that she had brought several spares.

Roxim went through two more handkerchiefs before his sneezing spasms finally stopped. "Much better," he said. "Now then, who's this that lent me the handkerchiefs? Somebody's new princess, eh?"

"We were discussing that when you came in," Kazul said, and turned to Cimorene. "You were saying? About cooking and so on."

"Couldn't I do that for one of you for a while?" Cimorene said.

The dragon smiled again, and Cimorene swallowed hard. "Possibly. Why would you want to do that?"

"Because then I wouldn't have to go home

and marry Therandil," Cimorene said. "Being a dragon's princess is a perfectly respectable thing to do, so my parents couldn't complain. And it would be much more interesting than embroidery and dancing lessons."

Several of the dragons made snorting or choking noises. Cimorene jumped, then decided that they were laughing.

"This is ridiculous," said a large, bright green dragon on Cimorene's left.

"Why?" asked Kazul.

"A princess volunteering? Out of the question!"

"That's easy for you to say," one of the other dragons grumbled. "You already have a princess. What about the rest of us?"

"Yes, don't be stuffy, Woraug," said another. "Besides, what else can we do with her?"

"Eat her," suggested the yellowish green dragon in a bored tone.

"No proper princess would come out looking for dragons," Woraug objected.

"Well, I'm not a proper princess, then," Cimorene snapped. "I make cherries jubilee, and I volunteer for dragons, and I conjugate Latin verbs – or at least I would if anyone would let me. So there!"

"Hear, hear," said the gray-green dragon.

"You see?" Woraug said. "Who would want an

improper princess?"

"I would," said Kazul.

"You can't be serious, Kazul," Woraug said irritably. "Why?"

"I like cherries jubilee," Kazul replied, still watching Cimorene. "And I like the look of her. Besides, the Latin scrolls in my library need cataloguing, and if I can't find someone who knows a little Latin, I'll have to do it myself."

"Give her a trial run first," a purplish green dragon advised.

Woraug snorted. "Latin and cherries jubilee! And for that you'd take on a black-haired, snippy little—"

"I'll thank you to be polite when you're discussing *my* princess," Kazul said, and smiled fiercely.

"Nice little gal," Roxim said, nodding approvingly and waving Cimorene's next-to-last handkerchief. "Got sense. Be good for you, Kazul."

"If that's settled, I'm going to go find a snack," said the yellowish green dragon.

Woraug looked around, but the other dragons seemed to agree with Roxim. "Oh, very well," Woraug said grumpily. "It's your choice, after all, Kazul."

"It certainly is. Now, Princess, if you'll come this way, I'll get you settled in."

Cimorene followed Kazul across the cave and down a tunnel. To her relief, the ball of light came with her. She had the uncomfortable feeling that if she had tried to walk behind Kazul in the dark, she would have stepped on her tail, which would not have been a good beginning.

Kazul led Cimorene through a long maze of tunnels and finally stopped in another cave. "Here we are," the dragon said. "You can use the small room on the right. I believe my last princess left most of the furnishings when she ran off with the knight."

"Thank you," Cimorene said. "When do I start my duties? And what are they, please?"

"You start right away," said Kazul. "I'll want dinner at seven. In the meantime, you can begin sorting the treasure." The dragon nodded toward a dark opening on the left. "I'm sure some of it needs repairing. There's at least one suit of armor with the leg off, and some of the cheaper magic swords are probably getting rusty. The rest of it really ought to be rearranged sensibly. I can never find anything when I want it."

"What about the library you mentioned?" Cimorene asked.

"We'll see how well you do on the treasure room first," Kazul said. "The rest of your job I'll explain as we go along. You don't object to learning a little magic, do you?"

"Not at all," said Cimorene.

"Good. It'll make things much easier. Go and wash up, and I'll let you into the treasure room so you can get started."

Cimorene nodded and went to the room Kazul had told her to use. As she washed her face and hands, she felt happier than she had in a long time. She was not going to have to marry Therandil, and sorting a dragon's treasure sounded far more interesting than dancing or embroidery. She was even going to learn some magic! And her parents wouldn't worry about her, once they found out where she was. For the first time in her life, Cimorene was glad she was a princess. She dried her hands and turned to go back into the main cave, wondering how best to persuade Kazul to help her brush up on her Latin. She didn't want the dragon to be disappointed in her skill.

"*Draco, draconem, dracone,*" she muttered, and her lips curved into a smile. She had always been rather good at declining nouns. Still smiling, she started forward to begin her new duties.

Cimorene settled in very quickly. She got along well with Kazul and learned her way around the caves with a minimum of mishaps. Actually, the caves were more like an intricate web of tunnels, connecting caverns of various shapes and sizes that belonged to individual dragons. It reminded Cimorene of an underground city with tunnels instead of streets. She had no idea how far the tunnels extended, though she rather suspected that some of them had been magicked, so that when you walked down them you went a lot farther than you thought you were going.

Kazul's section of the caves was fairly large. In addition to the kitchen – which was in a large cave near the exit, so that there wouldn't be a problem with the smoke from the fire – she had a sleeping cavern, three enormous treasure rooms at the far end of an intricate maze of twisty little passages, two even more enormous storage rooms for less valuable items, a library, a large bare cave for eating and visiting with other dragons, and the set of rooms assigned to Cimorene. All the caves smelled of dragon, a somewhat musty, smoky, cinnamony smell. Cimorene's first job was to air them out.

Cimorene's rooms consisted of three small connecting caves, just off Kazul's living cavern. They were furnished very comfortably in a mixture of styles and periods, and looked just like the guest rooms in most of the castles Cimorene had visited, only without windows.

They were much too small for a dragon to get inside. When asked, Kazul said that the dwarves had made them in return for a favor, and the dragon's tone prevented Cimorene from inquiring too closely into just what sort of favor it had been.

By the end of the first week, Cimorene was sure enough of her position to give Kazul a list of things that she needed in the kitchen. The previous princess – of whom Cimorene was beginning to have a very poor opinion – had apparently made do with a large skillet with three dents and wobbly handle, a wooden mixing bowl with a crack in it, a badly tarnished copper teakettle, and an assortment of mismatched plates, cups, and silverware, most of them chipped or bent.

Kazul seemed pleased by the request, and the following day Cimorene had everything she had asked for, except for a few of the more exotic pans and dishes. This made the cooking considerably easier and gave Cimorene more time to spend studying Latin and sorting treasure. The treasure was just as disorganized as Kazul had told her, and putting it in order was a major task. It was sometimes hard to tell whether a ring was enchanted, and Cimorene knew better than to put it on and see. It might be the sort of useful magic ring that turned you invisible, but it might also be the sort of ring that turned you into a frog. Cimorene did the best she could and kept a pile in the corner for things she was not sure about.

There was a great deal of treasure to be sorted. Most of it was stacked in one of the innermost caves in a large, untidy heap of crowns, rings, jewels, swords, and coins, but Cimorene kept finding things in other places as well, some of them quite unlikely. There was a small helmet under her bed (along with a great deal of dust), a silver bracelet set with opals on the reading table in the library, and two daggers and a jeweled ink pot behind the kitchen stove. Cimorene collected them all, along with the other things that were simply lying around in the halls, and put them back in the storerooms where they belonged, thinking to herself that dragons were clearly not very tidy creatures.

The first of the knights arrived at the end of the second week.

Cimorene was busy cleaning swords. Kazul had been right about their condition; not only were some of them rusty, but nearly all of them needed sharpening. She was polishing the last flakes of rust from an enormous broadsword when she heard someone calling from the mouth of the cave. Feeling somewhat irritated by the interruption, she rose and, carrying the sword, went to see who it was.

As she came nearer to the entrance, she was able to make out the words that whoever-it-was was shouting: "Dragon! Come out and fight! Fight for the Princess Cimorene of Linderwall!"

"Oh, honestly," Cimorene muttered, and quickened her step. "Here, you," she said as she came out into the sunlight. Then she had to duck as a spear flashed through the air over her head. "Stop that!" she cried. "I'm Princess Cimorene."

"You are?" said a doubtful voice. "Are you sure? I mean—"

Cimorene raised her head cautiously and squinted. It was still fairly early in the morning, and the sun was behind the person standing outside the cave, so that it was difficult to see anything but the outline of his figure against the brightness. "Of course I'm sure," Cimorene said. "What did you expect, letters of reference? Come around here where I can see who you are, please."

The figure moved sideways, and Cimorene saw that it was a knight in shiny new armor, except for the legs, where the armor was dusty from walking. Cimorene wondered briefly why he hadn't ridden, but decided not to ask. The knight's visor was raised, and a few wisps of sandy hair showed above his handsome face. He was studying her with an expression of worried puzzlement.

"What can I do for you?" Cimorene said after several moments had gone by and the knight still hadn't said anything.

"Well, um, if you *are* the Princess Cimorene, I've come to rescue you from the dragon," the knight said.

Cimorene set the point of the broadsword on the ground and leaned on it as if it were a walking cane. "I thought that might be it," she said. "But I'd rather not be rescued, thank you just the same."

"Not be rescued?" The knight's puzzled look deepened. "But princesses *always*—"

"No, they don't," Cimorene said firmly, recognizing the beginning of a familiar argument. "And even if I wanted to be rescued, you're going at it all wrong."

"What?" said the knight, thoroughly taken aback.

"Shouting, 'Come out and fight,' the way you did. No self-respecting dragon is going to answer to a challenge like that. It sounds like a child's dare. Dragons are very conscious of their dignity, at least all the ones I've met so far are."

"Oh dear," said the knight, sounding very

crestfallen. "What should I have said?"

"'Stand forth and do battle' is the usual challenge," Cimorene said with authority, remembering her princess lessons. She had always been more interested in what the knights and dragons were supposed to say than in memorizing the places where she was supposed to scream. "But the wording doesn't have to be exact as long as it's suitably formal. You're new at this, aren't you?"

"Rescuing you was going to be my first big quest," the knight said gloomily. "You're *sure* you don't want to be rescued?"

"Quite sure," Cimorene said. "I like living with Kazul."

"You *like*—" The knight stared at her for a moment. Then his expression cleared and he said, "Of course! The dragon's enchanted you. I should have thought of that before."

"Kazul has *not* enchanted me, and I do *not* want to be rescued by *anybody*," Cimorene said, alarmed by the knight's sudden enthusiasm. "This place suits me very well. I *like* polishing swords and cooking cherries jubilee and reading Latin scrolls. If you don't believe me, ask anyone in Linderwall. They've been complaining about my un-princesslike behavior for years."

"I did hear something about fencing lessons,"

the knight said doubtfully, "but knights aren't supposed to pay attention to that kind of thing. We're supposed to be above rumors and gossip."

"The fencing lessons were just the beginning," Cimorene assured him. "So you see why I'm perfectly happy being a dragon's princess."

"Um, yes," said the knight, but he did not look convinced. "Speaking of dragons, where's yours?"

"Kazul's not *my* dragon," Cimorene said sharply. "I'm *her* princess. You'll never have any luck dealing with dragons if you don't get these things straight. She's gone to the Enchanted Forest on the other side of the mountains to borrow a crêpe pan from a witch she knows."

"She's *what?*" said the knight.

"She's gone to borrow a crêpe pan," Cimorene repeated in a louder voice. "Perhaps you'd better have your helmet checked when you get back. They're not supposed to interfere with your hearing, but sometimes—"

"Oh, I heard you," the knight said. "But what does a dragon want with a crêpe pan?"

"She doesn't want it; I do. I found a recipe in the library that I want to try, and the kitchen just isn't equipped to handle anything but the most ordinary cooking. Kazul will fix that eventually, but for the time being we have to borrow things like crêpe pans and soufflé dishes."

"You really *do* like it here," the knight said wonderingly.

Cimorene refrained from replying that this was what she had been trying to tell him all along and instead said, "How did you know where I was?"

"Things get around." The knight waved a hand in a vague manner. "In fact, I had to hurry to make sure I was the first. Half of the Kingdom of Linderwall and a princess's hand in marriage is a reward rich enough to tempt a lot of people who wouldn't normally bother with this sort of thing."

"Father's offered half the kingdom to whoever rescues me?" Cimorene said incredulously. "That's more than all my sisters' dowries put together!"

"It's the usual thing in cases like this," the knight said mildly.

"It would be," Cimorene said in tones of deep disgust. "Well, at least you can go back and tell them I don't want to be rescued. Maybe that will keep anyone else from coming up here."

"I can't do that!" the knight said. "It's—"

"—just not done," Cimorene finished. "I understand perfectly." She gave him a polite farewell, more because she had been well brought up than because she felt like being polite, and sent him on his way. Then she went back into the cave and polished the broadsword until it was mirror-bright, which relieved her feelings a little.

There were two knights the following day, and four more the day after that. On the fourth day there was only one, but he was exceptionally stubborn, and it took Cimorene nearly two hours to get rid of him. By then she was thoroughly disgusted and even considered letting Kazul handle the knights from then on. She could not quite bring herself to do it. The knights would certainly attack Kazul as soon as they saw her, since that was what they were coming for, and sooner or later someone would get hurt. Cimorene did not like to think that someone might be hurt trying to rescue her, particularly since she did not want to be rescued, so with a sigh she decided that she would continue to handle the knights as long as Kazul would let her.

Prince Therandil showed up at the end of the third week. He was limping a little, as if his metal boots pinched his toes, and the feathers attached to the top of his helmet sagged badly. He stopped and carefully struck an impressive pose before issuing the usual challenge.

Cimorene was not in a mood to be impressed. Besides, she could see that his helmet was a different style from his gold armor and that the armor had gaps at the knees and elbows where it didn't fit together quite right.

"Aren't you a little slow?" she asked irritably. "There've been eight knights before you."

"Eight?" the prince said, frowning. "I thought by now there'd have been at least twelve. Perhaps I'd better come back later."

Cimorene stared at him in surprise. "Why?"

"Well, it would look better," Therandil explained seriously. "There's not much glory in defeating a dragon that hasn't already beaten ten or fifteen people at least. Sir Gorolax of Mirstwold won't even consider going after a dragon whose score is less than forty-five. I don't think I want to risk waiting that long, but eight just doesn't seem like enough."

"You're going to go away and wait until Kazul has defeated fifteen knights before you come back to rescue me?" Cimorene said. She found Therandil's smug confidence very annoying, but she didn't like to say so straight out.

"Not if you'd rather be rescued now, of course," Therandil said hastily. "Though you ought to consider the advantages, and I expect it won't be so very long . . ." His voice trailed off, and he looked at her hopefully.

"I'm afraid it will be a very long time," Cimorene said with satisfaction. "You see, Kazul hasn't defeated any knights at all yet."

"B-b-but I thought you said there'd been eight," Therandil spluttered.

"I said eight of them had come by; I didn't say they'd fought anybody. I sent them away."

"You *sent them away?*" Therandil repeated, plainly horrified. "But that's – that's—"

"—not done, I know." Cimorene smiled sweetly. "But I've done it. And I intend to go on doing it, so you might as well go home and warn your friends. They'd feel so foolish, you know, if they came all this way into the mountains to rescue me and then had to turn around and go back home without doing anything."

"They certainly would!" Therandil said indignantly. "What do you mean by playing these kinds of tricks? Don't you want to be rescued?"

"No," said Cimorene, losing her patience at last, "I don't. And I'm tired of having my work constantly interrupted. So please go away, and don't come back."

"You can't possibly mean that," Therandil said. "Besides, everyone expects me to rescue you."

"That's your problem," Cimorene told him. "I'm going to fix dinner. Goodbye." Before he could say anything else, she turned and ducked back into the cave, hoping the prince wouldn't follow.

CHAPTER 3

*In Which Cimorene Meets a Witch
and Has Doubts about a Wizard*

Therandil left, but he came back again the next day, and the day after that. It got so that Cimorene could not even step outside the cave without running into him. She might have been flattered if it hadn't been so obvious that Therandil was only worried about how foolish he'd look if he went home without fighting the dragon. On his fifth visit Cimorene was very sharp with him, and when he had not returned by mid-afternoon of the next day, she began to hope that he had finally left for good.

Cimorene was in the kitchen taking the pits out of cherries when she heard someone knocking at the mouth of the cave.

"Go *away*," she shouted in complete exasperation. "I've told you and told you, I don't want to be rescued, and I'm not going to argue with you any more!"

"I didn't come here to argue," said a no-nonsense female voice from outside. "I came to meet the person who keeps borrowing my crepe pan. It's not something there's normally much call for."

"Oh, dear," said Cimorene. She wiped her hands hastily on a corner of her apron and hurried out to greet her visitor. "I'm sorry," she said, coming around the gray rock at the cave mouth. "But I've been having a problem with knights lately, and I thought—" She stopped short as she got a good look at her caller for the first time.

The woman standing outside the cave was considerably shorter than Cimorene. Her ginger hair was piled in waves on top of her head. She had on a loose black robe with long sleeves, which she wore unbelted. A small pair of glasses with rectangular lenses sat firmly on her nose, and she carried an extremely twiggy broom in her left hand. Despite her unusual appearance, she projected an air of great self-assurance.

"I quite understand," she said, studying Cimorene shrewdly. "You must be Kazul's new princess."

"Yes, I'm Cimorene. And you are . . .?"

"Morwen," said the black-robed woman, leaning the broom against the rock. "Kazul and I have been friends for a long time, ever since I moved to the Enchanted Forest, so I thought I'd come have a look at her new princess."

"You're the person Kazul's been borrowing dishes from, aren't you?" Cimorene said, and blinked. "But then you must be—"

"A witch," Morwen finished. "I don't see why you find it surprising. It's not exactly an unusual profession in these parts."

"It's just that I haven't met one before," Cimorene said, not mentioning the fact that in Linderwall witches were considered dangerous and probably evil and were therefore avoided if at all possible. But then, people in Linderwall didn't like dragons much, either. "Won't you come in and have some tea?"

"I certainly will," said the witch, and she did. She prowled around like a nervous cat while Cimorene put the kettle on the stove and got out the tea things.

"Well," Morwen said approvingly as Cimorene filled the teapot, "you're the first princess I've ever met who has the sense to keep up with the kitchen."

Cimorene decided that she liked Morwen's down-to-earth manner. She soon found herself telling Morwen everything, from the fencing and philosophy and Latin lessons to the seemingly endless stream of knights. The story lasted through two cups of tea and finished with Therandil's stubborn insistence on rescuing her.

"That is absurd," Morwen said decidedly when Cimorene finished. "If this continues, you'll never get anything done."

"I know," Cimorene said. "I keep telling them I don't want to be rescued, but they're all so honorable that none of them will tell anyone when they go back because they think it would be gossiping."

"More likely they don't want to look foolish."

"Maybe, but even if they did tell people, I'm not sure anyone would believe it. I have a hard enough time convincing the knights when they show up in person."

"It's just as well that your visitors *have* been honorable," Morwen said, looking thoughtful. "Linderwall's a prosperous kingdom. Sooner or later the chance of getting hold of half of it is going to tempt someone to try rescuing you whether you want to be rescued or not."

"That hadn't occurred to me," Cimorene said with a worried frown. "What can I do about it?"

"I'm not sure," Morwen replied. "The situation's not at all usual, you know. I've never heard of a princess *volunteering* for a dragon before. Which rather surprises me, now that I think of it. A dragon's princess is practically guaranteed a good marriage, so you'd think princesses from the smaller kingdoms would be clamoring for the job."

"They're probably worried about being eaten," Cimorene said. "Do you think it would help if I sent my parents a letter?"

"Probably not," Morwen said after a moment's consideration. "But it can't hurt to try. I'll check my spell books when I get home. It may give me an idea. I suggest that you hunt through Kazul's library. She's been collecting scrolls for centuries; you ought to be able to find *something* useful. Meanwhile, we'll put up a sign."

"A sign?" Cimorene stared at Morwen for a moment, then began to smile. "'Road washed out,'" she said. "'Use alternate route.' Is that the kind of sign you were thinking of?"

"Exactly," Morwen said with approval. "It won't stop anyone who's really determined, but it will certainly slow them down. That should give us time to come up with something better."

The two women set to work at once and in a short time produced a large, official-looking sign. Morwen offered to set it up on her way back to the Enchanted Forest, but Cimorene thought it would be too awkward for her to carry while riding the broom. So, once Morwen had gone, Cimorene tucked the sign under her arm and started down the path.

Cimorene had not had a chance to do any real exploring before, though she had looked out at the mountains every day and wondered. She was happy to have an excuse to see more of the outside of her new home.

It was a lovely day, warm and sunny, and at first the path was level and easy. Cimorene was just beginning to wonder whether anyone would believe her sign, once she got it put up, when the path swung left around a boulder and narrowed to a tiny ledge that sloped steeply upward.

Cimorene stopped. Now she knew why none of the knights had ridden up to the cave. The ledge was barely wide enough for a person on foot to edge along sideways; the best rider in the world couldn't have got a horse down it. Cimorene rolled her sign up into a firm, tight cylinder and stuck it through her belt, so she would have her hands free while she climbed. Then she stepped out onto the ledge.

Sidling up the slope took a long time, for Cimorene was careful to make sure that each part of the ledge would hold before she trusted her weight to it. She was also careful not to look down. Heights had never bothered her before, but there was a big difference between standing solidly on top of a tower in Linderwall Castle behind a four-foot parapet and inching along a ledge barely six inches wide with nothing between her and a long fall.

She had almost reached the top of the slope, where the path widened again, when a portion of the ledge disappeared just ahead of her. Cimorene pulled her foot back and tried to figure out what had happened. She hadn't seen or heard the rock crumble and fall away; there was simply a two-foot gap in the ledge that hadn't been there before. She studied it for a moment, trying to think of a way of getting past. Nothing occurred to her. She felt a twinge of annoyance at the thought of all her wasted efforts, but cheered up at once when she realized that this would solve the problem of the visiting knights. If she couldn't get around or over the gap, an armored knight wouldn't be able to get by, either. Cimorene smiled and turned her head to creep back to safety.

There was another two-foot gap in the ledge on her other side. Cimorene frowned. Something very odd was going on, and she didn't like it.

"You look as if you are in need of assistance,"

said a deep voice from above her. "May I be of help?"

Cimorene turned her head and saw a man standing four feet away, on the path at the top of the ledge. He was tall and sharp-featured, and his eyes were a hard, bright black. Though he had a gray beard that reached nearly to his waist, his face did not look old. He wore loose robes made of blue and gray silk, and in one hand he held a staff as tall as himself made of dark, polished wood.

"Possibly," Cimorene answered. She was certain that the man was a wizard, though she had never met one before, and she did not want to agree to anything until she was sure of what she was agreeing to. The court philosopher had always claimed that wizards were very tricky. "May I know to whom I am speaking?"

"I am the wizard Zemenar," the man said. "And you must be Kazul's new princess. I hope you're not trying to run away. It's—"

"Not done," Cimorene said, feeling particularly annoyed because for once she was *not* doing anything improper. "Yes, I'm Cimorene."

"I was going to say that it isn't *wise* to run away from your dragon," the wizard corrected mildly. "I believe it's *done* all the time."

"I'm sorry," Cimorene said, but she didn't try to explain. "And I'm not running away, really I'm not. How did you know who I was?"

"It seemed unlikely that I would find any other charming young lady walking so casually through the Pass of Silver Ice," Zemenar answered. He smiled. "As you see, it is easy to find oneself in difficulties if one is not properly . . . prepared."

Cimorene decided that she didn't like him. He reminded her of one of her father's courtiers, a humorless, sneaky little man who had paid her compliments only when he was after something and who couldn't resist giving advice even when nobody wanted it. "The ledge was all here when I started," she said. An idea crossed her mind, and she looked hard at Zemenar. "I don't suppose *you* know what happened to the two missing bits?"

A flash of startled annoyance crossed the wizard's face; then his expression smoothed back into pleasant politeness. He shrugged. "The Pass of Silver Ice is a strange place. Odd things frequently occur."

"Not like this," Cimorene muttered. She was sure, now, that the wizard had made the ledge vanish so that he could pretend to rescue her, but she had no idea why he would want her to think she owed him a favor. Actually, it surprised her that he had destroyed the ledge. She didn't think the dragons would be too happy when they found out. Unless he hadn't really destroyed it.

"What did you say?" Zemenar said, frowning uncertainly.

Cimorene ignored him. Without looking down, she slid her right foot along the ledge. The rock felt firm and solid. Slowly she transferred her weight and brought her left foot up beside her right. She shifted again, still careful not to look down, and slid her right foot forward once again.

"What are you doing?" Zemenar demanded.

"Getting off this ledge," Cimorene replied. "I should think that was obvious." One more step would bring her to the path, but Zemenar was squarely in her way. "Would you mind moving back a little so I'll have somewhere to stand?"

Zemenar's eyes narrowed, but he backed up several paces, and Cimorene stepped onto the path. She wanted to heave a sigh of relief, but she did not. She wasn't going to let Zemenar have the satisfaction of knowing she had been worried. Instead, she gave him her best royal smile and said with polite insincerity, "Thank you for offering to help, but as you see, it wasn't needed. Do stop by and visit some time."

"I will," Zemenar said, as if he meant it. "And a very good day to you, Princess Cimorene."

With that he vanished. There was no smoke

or fire or whirlwind. There wasn't even a shimmer in the air as he disappeared. He was simply and suddenly gone.

Cimorene stared at the place where the wizard had been and felt a shiver run down her spine. It took a very powerful wizard indeed to vanish so quietly. And she still didn't know what he wanted.

She shook herself and started down the path. She would worry about the wizard later; right now she had to find a place to put up her sign so she could get back to the cave. She didn't feel much like exploring any more.

She hadn't taken more than two or three steps when a dark shadow passed over her. Looking up, startled, she saw a flash of yellow-green scales. An instant later a dragon landed on the path in front of her, blocking the way completely. His tail hung over the edge, and he had to keep his wings partly unfurled in order to stay in balance. Cimorene recognized him at once. It was the yellow-green dragon who had wanted to eat her the day she arrived so unexpectedly in the dragons' cave.

"I saw the whole thing," the dragon said with nasty, triumphant glee. "Running away — and talking to a wizard! Just wait until Kazul hears. She'll be sorry she didn't just let us eat you and be done with it."

"I offer you greetings and good fortune on your travels," Cimorene said, figuring that it was best to be polite to anyone as large and toothy as a dragon, even if he wasn't being at all polite to her. "I'm not running away."

"Then what are you doing? Kazul doesn't have any business that would bring you down this side of the pass."

"I came out to put up a sign to keep the knights away," Cimorene said.

"That's ridiculous." The dragon sniffed. "I've been on patrol in this part of the mountains for the past week, and I haven't seen or smelled even a hint of a knight."

"You haven't been by Kazul's cave, then," Cimorene said. "At least nine of them have shown up there in the past week. Though for the past couple of days it's been mostly a prince."

"Princes don't smell any different from knights, and I'd have noticed if any of them were hanging around," the dragon said flatly. "And what about that wizard you were talking to?"

"Chaaarrge!" shouted a familiar voice from the other side of the dragon.

"Therandil!" Cimorene shouted. "I told you to go *away!*"

The yellow-green dragon twisted his long

neck and glanced back over his shoulder. He seemed to bunch together like a cat crouching. Then he sprang straight up into the air, and Cimorene was blinded by the cloud of dust raised by the flapping of his enormous wings. She had the presence of mind to flatten herself back against the rocks by the side of the path, and a moment later she heard someone blundering by. She stuck out a foot.

"Ow!" she said as Therandil fell over with a clatter. She'd forgotten that he'd be wearing iron boots along with the rest of his armor.

"Cimorene? Is that you?" Therandil said.

"Of course it's me," Cimorene replied, rubbing her ankle. "Open your eyes; the dust's settled." She looked up as she spoke and saw the dragon soar out of sight behind a cliff.

"I'm sorry," Therandil said, and then in an anxious tone he added, "I hope I didn't hurt you, stumbling into you like that."

Cimorene started to say that it was nothing and that it had been her fault anyway, when she suddenly got a much better idea. "I think you've sprained my ankle," she declared.

"Oh, no," Therandil said. He sounded truly dismayed, though Cimorene couldn't see his face because he was wearing his helmet with the visor down.

"I probably won't be able to walk for at least a

month," she declared. "And there's certainly no way I can climb down this mountain."

"But if you can't walk—" Therandil said, and paused. Then he squared his shoulders and went on, "—then I suppose I'll have to carry you." He didn't sound as if he liked the idea.

"I don't think that would work very well," Cimorene said quickly. "How will you fight when all the dragons come back if you're carrying me? No, you'll have to leave me here and go back alone."

"You can't stay here!" Therandil protested, though Cimorene's talk of *when all the dragons come back* had plainly made him nervous.

"I have to," Cimorene said, trying to sound noble and long-suffering. "The dragons will make sure I get safely back to Kazul's cave, and a month isn't too long a wait, after all."

"I don't understand," Therandil said, and he did look thoroughly puzzled.

"There's no point in you or anyone else coming up here to rescue me for at least a month, not till my ankle's better," Cimorene explained patiently.

"Oh, I see," Therandil said. He tilted his head back and scanned the empty sky. "You're quite sure you'll be all right? Then I'll just be going before those dragons return." He turned and started down the path as quickly as he could manage in full armor.

CҺAPTER 4

In Which Kazul Has a Dinner Party, and Cimorene Makes Dessert

Cimorene watched Therandil go with feelings of great relief. Now she had at least a month to find a permanent way of discouraging the knights, for she was quite certain that Therandil would spread the news of her "injury." She decided to put up her sign anyway, just in case, and after a little looking she found a scrubby tree beside the path and hung the sign on it.

On her way back to Kazul's cave, she noticed that the two pieces of the ledge were still invisible, and she was very careful about crossing them. She looked down once, out of curiosity, and was immediately sorry. She was not comfortable with the sight of her own feet firmly planted on nothing at all, with the sharp, spiky tops of spruce trees in full view some fifty feet below.

Kazul arrived only a few minutes after Cimorene herself. Cimorene was looking for some thread to mend her skirts (which had got torn and stained while she was climbing along the ledge) when she heard the unmistakable sounds of a dragon sliding into the main cave.

"Cimorene?" Kazul's voice called.

"Coming," Cimorene called back, abandoning her search. She picked up her lamp and hurried out to greet Kazul.

"I'm glad to see you're still here," Kazul said mildly as Cimorene came into the large cave. "Moranz was quite sure you'd run off with a knight or a wizard. I couldn't make out for certain which."

"Is Moranz the yellow-green dragon who wanted to eat me?" Cimorene asked. "Because if he is, he's just trying to make trouble."

"I'm well aware of that," Kazul said with a sigh that sent a burnt-bread smell halfway across the cave. "But things would be easier for me if you didn't provide him with any material to make trouble with. Exactly what happened?"

"Well, Morwen came to visit this afternoon," Cimorene began. "We were talking about all the . . . interruptions I've been having, and she suggested putting up a sign . . ." She explained why she had gone to put up the sign herself and told Kazul in detail about her meetings with the wizard, the dragon, and the prince.

"So Morwen was here," Kazul said. She sat back, and the scales on her tail rattled comfortably against the floor. "That simplifies matters. Did you bring the sign back with you?"

"No, I found a tree and hung it by the path," Cimorene said, wondering what this was all about. "In case Therandil doesn't tell everyone about my ankle after all."

"Better still," Kazul said, and smiled fiercely, showing all her teeth. "Moranz is going to regret meddling."

"Meddling in what?"

"My business."

"I'd like a little more of an explanation than that, if you don't mind giving one," Cimorene said with a touch of exasperation.

Kazul looked startled, then thoughtful. Then she nodded. "I keep forgetting that you're not as empty-headed as most princesses," she said. "Sit down and make yourself comfortable. This may take a while."

Cimorene found a rock and sat on it. Kazul settled into a more restful position, folded her wings neatly along her back, and began. "It has to do with status. Dragons aren't required to have princesses, you see. Most of us don't. There are never enough to go around, and some of us prefer not to have to deal with the annoyances that come with them."

"Knights," Cimorene guessed.

"Among other things," Kazul said, nodding. "So having a princess in residence has become a minor mark of high status among dragons."

"A *minor* mark?"

Kazul smiled. "I'm afraid so. It's the equivalent of, oh, serving expensive imported fruit at dinner. It's a nice way of showing everyone how rich you are, but you could make just as big an impression by having some of those fancy pastries with the smooth glazed icing and spunsugar roses."

"I see." Cimorene did see, though she found herself wishing that Kazul had found something else to compare it to. The talk of dinner reminded her too much of Moranz's repeated desire to eat her.

"Moranz is young and not very bright, I'm afraid," Kazul said, almost as if she had read Cimorene's mind. "He seems to have the mistaken impression that if a princess behaves badly, it reflects on the dragon who captured her. Possibly it comes from his inability to keep any of his own princesses for more than a week.

Some of the lesser dragons were very snide about it when he lost his third one in a row. I believe she sneaked out while he was napping."

"I don't see how he can blame his princesses," Cimorene objected. "I mean, if most princesses are unwilling, it must be fairly usual for them to try to get away."

"Of course, but Moranz doesn't see it that way. He's been trying to catch someone else's princess in a similar foolishness for years, and he's quite sure he's finally done so. He's undoubtedly spreading the story of your escape far and wide at this very minute."

"Oh, dear," said Cimorene.

Kazul smiled again, and her teeth glittered silver in the lamplight. "He'll look extremely foolish when it becomes obvious that you're still here. Which is one reason I've asked a few of my friends to dinner tonight."

"You've *what?*" Cimorene said. All her worries about Moranz were instantly replaced by worries about fixing dinner on short notice for an unknown number of dragons. "How many? What time will they be here? Where are we going to *put* them all?"

"Six. Around eight-thirty. In the banquet cave. And you won't be doing anything but dessert. I've already arranged for the rest of the meal."

"Arranged? With whom?"

"Ballimore the giantess. She's loaned me the Cauldron of Plenty that she uses when her twelve-headed son-in-law drops in for dinner unannounced. It'll handle most things, but all it can produce in the way of dessert is burned mint custard and sour-cream-and-onion ice cream."

"Ugh!" said Cimorene. "I see your problem."

"Exactly. Can you manage?"

"Not if you want cherries jubilee," Cimorene said, frowning. "I haven't got a pot large enough to make seven dragons' worth of cherries jubilee. Would chocolate mousse do? I can make two or three batches, and there should be time for all of them to chill if you're not starting until eight-thirty."

"Chocolate mousse will be fine," Kazul assured her. "Come along and I'll show you where to bring it."

Cimorene picked up a lamp and followed Kazul into the public tunnels that surrounded Kazul's private caves. She was a little surprised, but when she saw the size of the banquet cave, she understood. It was enormous. Fifty or sixty dragons, perhaps even a hundred of them, would fit into it quite comfortably. Obviously it had to be a public room; there simply wasn't enough space under the Mountains of Morning for every dragon to have a cave this size.

Kazul made sure Cimorene could find her way to the banquet cave without help and then left her in the kitchen to melt slabs of chocolate and whip gallons of cream for the mousse. By the time she finished, she was hot and tired, and all she really wanted to do was to take a nap. But Kazul was expecting her to serve the mousse, and Cimorene wasn't about to appear before all those dragons in her old clothes with sweaty straggles of hair sticking to her neck and a smear of chocolate across her nose, so instead of napping, she pumped a cauldron of water, heated it on the kitchen fire, and took a bath.

Once she was clean she felt much better. She checked to make sure the mousse was setting properly, then went into her own rooms to decide what she should wear. Unfortunately, she was afraid she didn't have much choice. The wardrobe in her bedroom was full of neat, serviceable dresses suitable for cooking in or rummaging through treasure, but the only dressy clothes she had were the ones she had arrived in. She got them out of the back of the wardrobe and found to her dismay that the hem of the gown was badly stained with mud from her long walk. There was no time to clean it; she would have to wear one of the everyday dresses.

With a sigh Cimorene turned back to the

wardrobe and opened it once more to look for the nicest of the ordinary clothes. She gasped in surprise. The hangers were now full of the most beautiful gowns she had ever seen. Some were silk, and some were velvet; some were heavy brocade, and some were layers of feather-light gauze; some were embroidered with gold or silver, and some were sewn with jewels.

"Well, of course," Cimorene said aloud after a stunned moment. "Why would a dragon have an ordinary wardrobe? Of *course* it's magic. What's in it depends on what I'm looking for."

One of the wardrobe doors waggled slightly, and its hinges creaked in smug agreement. Cimorene blinked at it, then shook herself and began looking through the gowns.

She chose one of red velvet, heavily embroidered with gold, and found matching slippers in the bottom of the obliging wardrobe. She let her black hair hang in loose waves nearly to her feet and even dug her crown out of the back of the drawer where she'd stuffed it on her first night. She finished getting ready a few minutes early. Feeling very cheerful, she went to the kitchen to fetch the mousse.

It took Cimorene four trips to get the mousse down to the serving area just off the banquet cave. A dragon-sized serving was a little over a bucketful, and she could barely manage to carry two at a time. When everything was ready, she stood in the serving area and waited nervously for Kazul to ring for dessert. She could hear the muffled booming of the dragons' voices through the heavy oak door, but she could not make out what any of them were saying.

The bell rang at last, summoning Cimorene to serve dessert. She carried the mousse into the banquet cavern, two servings at a time, and set it in front of Kazul and her guests. The dragons were crouched around a shoulder-high slab of white stone. Cimorene had to be very careful about lifting the mousse up onto it. Fortunately, she didn't have to wonder which dragon to serve first. She could tell which dragons were most important from their places at the table, and she made a silent apology to her protocol teacher, who had insisted that she learn about seating arrangements. (Protocol had been one of the princess lessons Cimorene had hated most.)

As she set the last serving in front of Kazul, one of the other dragons said in a disgruntled and vaguely familiar voice, "I see the rumors are wrong again, Kazul. Or did you have to go after her and haul her back the way the rest of us do?"

Cimorene turned angrily, but before she

could say anything, a large gray-green dragon on the other side of the stone slab said, "Nonsense, Woraug! Girl's got more sense than that. You shouldn't listen to gossip. Next thing you know, you'll be chasing after that imaginary wizard Gaurim's been on about." Cimorene recognized the speaker at once. He was Roxim, the elderly dragon she had given four of her handkerchiefs to.

"I suppose it was that idiot Moranz again, trying to cause trouble," a purple-green dragon said with bored distaste. "Someone should do something about him."

"Kazul still hasn't answered my question," Woraug said, and his tail lashed once like the tail of an angry cat. "And I'd like her to do so if the rest of you will stop sidetracking the conversation."

"Here, now!" Roxim said indignantly. "That's a bit strong, Woraug! Too strong, if you ask me."

"I didn't," Woraug said. "I asked Kazul. And I'm still waiting."

"I'm very pleased with my princess," Kazul said mildly. "And no, I didn't have to haul her back, as you would realize if you'd given the matter a little thought. Or does your princess normally leave seven servings of chocolate mousse in the kitchen when she runs away?"

"Hear, hear!" Roxim said.

Cimorene noted with interest that Woraug's scales had turned an even brighter shade of green than normal and that he was starting to smell faintly of brimstone.

"One of these days you'll go too far, Kazul," he said.

"You started it," Kazul pointed out. She turned to the gray dragon. "What's this about Gaurim and a wizard, Roxim?"

"You haven't heard?" Roxim said, sounding surprised. "Gaurim's been raving about it for weeks. Somebody snuck into her cave and stole a book from her library. No traces, but for some reason she's positive it was a wizard. *Achoo!*" Roxim sneezed, emitting a ball of flame that just missed hitting his bowl of mousse. "Gives me an allergy attack just thinking about it."

"If it wasn't a wizard, who was it?" the dragon at the far end of the table asked.

"Could have been anybody – an elf, a dwarf, even a human," Roxim responded. "No reason to think it was a wizard just because Gaurim didn't catch him in the act. Not with the amount of time she spends away from home."

"Which book did she lose?" said the thin, brownish green dragon next to Kazul.

"What does it matter?" the purple-green dragon muttered.

"Some history or other. And that's another

thing — what would a wizard want with a history book? No, no, Gaurim's making a lot of fuss over a common thief. That's what I say."

"It could have been a wizard," said the dragon at the far end. "Who knows why they want the things they want?"

"Ridiculous!" Roxim replied with vigor. "A wizard wouldn't dare come through this part of the mountains. They know what we'd do to 'em, by George! Beg pardon," he added to the silver-green dragon next to him, who appeared to have been rather shocked by his language.

"I'm afraid you're wrong there," Kazul said. "Cimorene met one today, less than a two-minute flight from my cave."

"What? What?" Roxim said. "You're sure?"

"That's done it." The purple-green dragon rolled his head in an irritated gesture, so that his scales made a scratching noise as they rubbed together. "You'll never get him to quit talking about it now."

"Quite sure," Cimorene assured Roxim, after glancing at Kazul to make sure she was expected to answer Roxim's question for herself. "He made two bits of the ledge I was standing on turn invisible so I would think it wasn't safe to keep going."

"Certainly sounds like a wizard to me," the dragon at the far end commented.

"What did he look like?" asked the silver-green dragon.

Cimorene described the wizard as well as she could, then added, "He said his name was Zemenar."

"Zemenar? That's ridiculous!" Woraug snorted. "Zemenar was elected head of the Society of Wizards last year. He wouldn't waste his time playing games with somebody's princess."

"Not unless he had a great deal to gain by it," the thin dragon said in a thoughtful tone. She turned her head and looked speculatively at Cimorene.

"Such as?" Woraug said. He waited a moment, but no one answered. "No, I can't believe it was Zemenar. The girl's made a mistake; that's all."

"Perhaps it wasn't him," Cimorene said, holding on to her temper as hard as she could. "I've never met Zemenar, so I wouldn't know. But that's who he said he was."

"And wouldn't it be amusing if she were right?" the purple-green dragon said, showing some interest in the proceedings for the first time.

"I don't see that it matters," the silver-green dragon said. "The important thing is that he was a wizard, poking around smack in the middle of our mountains. What are we going to do about it?"

"Tell King Tokoz," Roxim said. "His job to handle this sort of thing, isn't it?"

"What can Tokoz do about it?" Woraug said, and there was a faint undercurrent of contempt in his tone.

"He could use the King's Crystal to find out what the wizards are really doing," the thin dragon said in a prim tone.

"He won't use the crystal for anything less than a full-fledged war," Woraug said. "And why should he? What could Tokoz do even if he did find out some wizard was preying on poor defenseless dragons like Gaurim?"

"Lodge a formal protest with the Society of Wizards," Roxim answered promptly, ignoring Woraug's sarcasm. "Proper thing to do, no question. Then the next time anyone sees a wizard . . ." His voice trailed off, and he snapped his teeth together suggestively.

"He'd probably just set up a committee," the purple-green dragon said. "Can't anyone think of something else?"

"I don't think we should do anything until we have some idea what Zemenar was after," said the thin dragon. "It could be important."

"We have to do something!" the silver-green dragon said. Her claws clashed against the stone table. "We can't have wizards wandering in and out whenever they please! Why, we'd lose half our magic in no time."

"Not to mention everyone sneezing themselves silly every time one of those dratted staffs gets too close," added the dragon at the far end.

The dragons began arguing among themselves about what to do and how best to do it. It reminded Cimorene of the way her father's ministers argued. Everyone seemed to agree that something ought to be done about the wizards, but they each had a different idea about what was appropriate. Roxim insisted huffily that the only thing to do was to inform the King, who would then make a formal protest. The thin dragon wanted to find out what the wizards were up to (she didn't say how this was to be done) before anyone tried to chase them off. The silver-green dragon wanted patrols sent out immediately to eat any wizard who ventured into the Mountains of Morning. The dragon at the far end of the table wanted to attack the headquarters of the Society of Wizards the following morning, and the purple-green dragon thought it would be most entertaining to wait and see what the wizards did next. Woraug was the only one of the guests who did not have a proposal, though he made occasional comments, usually sarcastic ones, about everyone else's suggestions.

Kazul did not say anything at all. Cimorene was at first surprised and then puzzled by her silence, since Kazul was the one who had set the whole discussion going to begin with. As the argument grew more heated, however, Cimorene began to be glad that there was at least one dragon present who was not involved in it. The dragon at the far end of the table was starting to breathe little tongues of fire at the purple-green dragon, and Roxim was threatening loudly to have another allergy attack, but Cimorene was fairly sure that Kazul would stop the discussion before things got completely out of hand.

She was right. A moment later, while the dragon at the far end was taking a deep breath to continue arguing and the thin dragon was winding up a long, involved train of logical reasons why her proposal was the best, Kazul said, "Thank you all for your advice. I'll certainly think about it before I decide what to do."

"What do you mean by that?" the thin dragon asked suspiciously.

"It was my princess who met the wizard," Kazul pointed out. "Therefore, it is my decision whether to report the matter to the King, or to take some action on my own, or to ask for co-operation from some of you."

None of the other dragons appeared to like hearing this, but to Cimorene's surprise none of them gave Kazul any argument about it. The dragon at the far end of the table made a few half-hearted grumbles, but that was all, and the conversation turned to the intricacies of several draconian romances that were currently in progress. As soon as her guests appeared to have calmed down, Kazul gave the signal for the empty mousse dishes to be taken away, so Cimorene only heard a few incomprehensible snatches of the new conversation. She did not really mind. She had plenty to think about already.

CHAPTER 5

In Which Cimorene Receives a Formal Call from Her Companions in Dire Captivity

Kazul slept late the following morning, and Cimorene was afraid that she would leave before Cimorene had a chance to ask about the dragons' after-dinner conversation. To her relief, Kazul called her in as soon as she was thoroughly awake and asked Cimorene to bring in the brushes for cleaning her scales.

"What was that crystal your friend mentioned last night?" Cimorene asked as she laid out the brushes. "The one she thought King Tokoz could use somehow to find out what the wizards are doing?"

"The King's Crystal?" Kazul said. "It's one of

the magical objects that belongs to the King of the Dragons."

"But what does it *do?* And why did Woraug think that King Tokoz wouldn't want to use it?"

"Using the crystal is difficult and tiring, and Tokoz is getting old," Kazul replied. "Zareth was right to say that the crystal ought to be used, but it will take more evidence than we have right now to persuade the King of that. As to what it does, the crystal shows things that are happening in other times and places. It's useful, but it can be very difficult to interpret correctly."

"Oh, a crystal ball," Cimorene said, nodding. She tapped Kazul's side, and the dragon bent her elbow so that the scales were easier to reach. "The court wizard at Linderwall had one, but I had to stop my magic lessons before he got a chance to show me how to work it."

"The King's Crystal is more like a plate, but the principle is the same?" Kazul said.

"A crystal plate?" Cimorene blinked. "No wonder nobody talks about it much. It just doesn't sound right."

Kazul shrugged. "The King's Crystal is much more accurate than an ordinary crystal ball, and if 'crystal plate' sounds odd to most people, it means that fewer of them will try to steal it."

"Was that what the silver-green dragon meant

when he said that if the wizards started wandering through the mountains you'd lose half your magic in no time? I never heard that wizards stole magic rings and swords and things."

"Not magic things," Kazul said. "*Magic*. Wizards steal magic. That's where their power comes from."

"How can a wizard steal magic?" Cimorene said sceptically. She climbed on a stool and began working at the ribs of Kazul's wings.

"Wizards' staffs absorb magic from whatever happens to be nearby," Kazul said, stretching out her left wing so Cimorene could get at the base. "That's why they're always hanging around places like the Mountains of Morning and the Enchanted Forest. The more magic there is in the area, the more their staffs can soak up."

"What would happen if someone stole a wizard's staff? Would the wizard still be able to use it?"

"The wizard wouldn't be able to work any magic until he got it back," Kazul said. "Most of them have a great many anti-theft spells on their staffs for exactly that reason. Of course, it happens anyway, now and then. And as long as the wizard and the staff are separated, the staff doesn't absorb magic."

"It doesn't sound like a very good arrangement to me," Cimorene said. "I can think of half a dozen ways a staff could be lost or forgotten or stolen or something. It doesn't seem sensible for a wizard to depend so much on anything that's so easy to mislay."

Kazul shrugged. "They seem to like it."

"I can see why you don't want them in your part of the mountains."

"Can you? Do you have any idea how unpleasant it is to have part of your essence sucked out of you without so much as a by-your-leave? Not to mention the side effects."

"Side effects?" Cimorene said, puzzled.

"There! Turn around, and I'll do your other side."

"Roxim isn't the only dragon who's allergic to wizards," Kazul said dryly as she shifted her position. "Or rather, to their staffs. We all are. Roxim's just a little more sensitive than most. That's why we made the agreement with them in the first place."

"The dragons have an agreement with the wizards?"

Kazul nodded. "To be precise, the King of the Dragons has an agreement with the head of the Society of Wizards: the wizards stay out of our portions of the Mountains of Morning, and we allow them partial access to the Caves of

Fire and Night. At least, that's the way it's supposed to work. King Tokoz is getting old and forgetful, and lately wizards have been turning up in all sorts of places they aren't supposed to be."

"Like that wizard Zemenar I met on the path," Cimorene said. "Do you think he really *was* the same Zemenar that's the head of the Society of Wizards?"

"I doubt that anyone, even another wizard, would dare impersonate him," Kazul said. "He has a nasty reputation."

Cimorene remembered the hard black eyes and sharp features of the wizard she had met. He had certainly looked nasty enough, even when he was pretending to be nice. He was sneaky, too, or he wouldn't have tried to trick her. And he had been very annoyed when Cimorene got off the ledge without his help. Cimorene frowned.

"I wonder what he wanted, really," she mused. "Do you suppose he'll stop by the way he said he would?"

"I almost wish he would try," Kazul said. There was an angry glint in her eye, and her claws made a scratching sound against the stone floor of the cave as she flexed them.

"Don't wiggle," Cimorene said. "If Zemenar is as tricky as everyone says, he won't come while you're here. He'll wait until you've gone somewhere and I'm alone."

"True." Kazul frowned. Then she looked at Cimorene, and her eyes took on a speculative gleam. "He probably thinks you're as silly as most princesses, so he'll be hoping to trick you into giving him whatever it is he's after. And if he does—"

"Then maybe I can fool him instead," Cimorene finished. "And once we know what he's after, we can decide what to do about it."

Kazul and Cimorene discussed this idea while Cimorene finished brushing the dragon's scales. There was very little they could do to prepare since they did not know when Zemenar might show up at the cave or what he might do when he arrived. Then Kazul went off to inspect the ledge where Cimorene had met the wizard, to see whether bits of it were still invisible.

When Kazul had gone, Cimorene went into the library to hunt through all the books and scrolls of spells. The behavior of the dragons at dinner the previous evening had made a considerable impression on her, and she wanted to see whether she could find a spell to fireproof herself. Until then she hadn't realized that when a dragon lost his temper, he started breathing fire. Not that she was planning to do anything to irritate Kazul – or any other dragon, for that matter – but the dragons at dinner had been too annoyed to be careful, and she didn't want to get burned by accident, no matter how sorry the dragon might be afterward.

At first Cimorene didn't have much luck. She hadn't had time to do much organizing in the library, and most of the books and scrolls were lying in haphazard, dust-covered piles. Some had even fallen onto the floor, and there were spiders everywhere. Cimorene realized that if she wanted to find anything, she was going to have to do some more cleaning first. With a sigh she went to get a bucket of water, some cloths for washing and dusting, and a handkerchief to tie over her hair.

She worked for several hours, dusting books and manuscripts, wiping off the dirty bookshelves, and putting the books back in neat rows when the shelves were dry. She found two books and five old scrolls that looked as if they might be interesting. These she set on one of the tables to look at later. She had just pulled a stained and yellowed stack of papers out of the back of the second-to-last bookshelf when she heard someone hallooing outside.

"Now what?" she muttered crossly. She set the papers on the table with the rest of the books she was planning to look at later and went out to see who was there.

To her surprise, the noise was coming from the back entrance, not from the mouth of the cave. She hurried into the passage, rounded the corner, and found herself facing three beautiful, elegantly dressed princesses. They were all blonde and blue-eyed and slender, and several inches shorter than Cimorene. The first one wore a gold crown set with diamonds, and her hair was the color of sun-ripened wheat. The second wore a silver crown set with sapphires, and her hair was the color of crystallized honey. The last wore a pearl-covered circlet, and her hair was the color of ripe apricots. They looked rather taken aback by the sight of Cimorene in her dust-covered dress and kerchief.

"Oh, bother," Cimorene said under her breath. Then she smiled her best smile and said, "Welcome to the caves of the dragon Kazul. May I help you with anything?"

"We have made the perilous journey through the tunnels to see the Princess Cimorene, newly come to these caverns, to comfort her and together bemoan our sad and sorry fates," the first princess said haughtily. "Tell her we are here."

"I'm Cimorene," Cimorene said. "I don't need comforting, and I'm not particularly sad or sorry to be here, but if you'd like to come in and have some tea, you're welcome to."

The first two princesses looked as if they would have liked to be startled and appalled by this announcement but were much too well bred to show what they were feeling. The princess with the pearl circlet looked surprised and rather intrigued, and she glanced hopefully at her companions. They ignored her, but after a moment the first princess said grandly, "Very well, we will join you, then," and swept past Cimorene into the cave.

The other princesses followed, the one with the pearl circlet giving Cimorene a shy smile as she passed. Cimorene, wondering what she had got herself into, brought up the rear. The princesses stopped when they reached the main cave, and the ones in the gold and silver crowns looked a bit disgruntled. The one in the pearl circlet stared in unabashed amazement. "My goodness," she said, "you certainly do have a lot of space."

"Alianora!" the gold-crowned princess said sharply, and the princess with the pearl circlet flushed and subsided, looking unhappy.

"This way," Cimorene said hastily, and led the three princesses into the kitchen. "Do sit down," she said, waving at the bench beside the kitchen table.

The gold-crowned princess looked at the bench with distaste, but after a moment she sat down. The other two followed her example. There was a brief silence while Cimorene filled the copper tea-kettle and hung it over the fire, and then the gold-crowned princess said, "I am remiss in my duties, for I have not yet told you who we are. I am the Princess Keredwel of the Kingdom of Raxwel, now captive of the dread dragon Gornul. This" – she nodded toward the princess in the silver crown – "is the Princess Hallanna of the Kingdom of Poranbuth, now captive of the dread dragon Zareth. And this" – she waved at the girl in the pearl circlet – "is the Princess Alianora of the Duchy of Toure-on-Marsh, now prisoner of the dread dragon Woraug."

"Pleased to meet you," Cimorene said. "I am Princess Cimorene of the Kingdom of Linder-wall, now princess of the dragon Kazul. What sort of tea would you like? I have blackberry, ginger, chamomile, and gunpowder green. I'm afraid I used the last of the lapsang souchong this morning."

"Blackberry, please," Keredwel said. She gave Cimorene a considering look. "You seem to be most philosophic about your fate."

"Would that I had so valiant a spirit," Hallanna said in failing accents. "But my sensibility is too great, I fear, for me to follow your example."

"If you don't like being a dragon's princess, why don't you escape?" Cimorene asked, remembering that Kazul had said that three princesses in a row had run away from the yellow-green dragon, Moranz.

Keredwel and Hallanna looked shocked. "Without being rescued?" Hallanna faltered. "Walk all that way, with dragons and trolls and goodness knows what else hiding in the rocks, ready to eat me? Oh, I *couldn't!*"

"It isn't done," Keredwel said coldly. "And I notice that *you* haven't tried it."

"But I'm enjoying being Kazul's princess," Cimorene said cheerfully. "I suppose I might have been upset if I'd been carried off the way you were, but I can hardly complain as it is, can I?"

Alianora leaned forward. "Then you really *did* volunteer to be Kazul's princess?"

Keredwel and Hallanna turned and stared at their companion. "*Where* did you get *that* ridiculous idea, Alianora?" Hallanna said.

"W-Woraug said—" Alianora faltered.

"You must have misunderstood," Keredwel said severely. "*No one* volunteers to be a dragon's princess. It isn't *done.*"

"Actually, Alianora's quite right," Cimorene said as she set the teacups in front of her visitors. "I did volunteer." She smiled sweetly at the thunderstruck expressions on the faces of the first two princesses. "I got tired of embroidery and etiquette."

Keredwel and Hallanna seemed unsure of how to take this announcement, so they made polite conversation about the tea and asked Cimorene questions about the current fashions. Alianora didn't say very much, and the few times she tried either Keredwel or Hallanna jumped on her. Cimorene felt rather sorry for Alianora.

The princesses swept off at last, still somewhat puzzled by Cimorene's attitude. Cimorene gave a sigh of relief and set about cleaning up the kitchen. She was just rinsing the last of the cups when she heard someone hesitantly clearing her throat behind her. Cimorene turned and saw Alianora standing timidly in the doorway.

"Hello again," Cimorene said. "Did you forget something?"

"Not exactly," Alianora said. "I mean, I told Keredwel I did, but actually I just wanted to get away from them for a while. I hope you don't mind."

"I don't mind at all as long as you don't expect more hospitality," Cimorene assured her. "I have to get back to work on the library."

"What are you doing?" Alianora asked. She seemed really interested, so Cimorene explained about the fireproofing spell.

"It sounds like a wonderful idea," Alianora said when Cimorene finished. "The dragons are careful around us, but it would be nice not to have to depend on them not to lose their tempers." She hesitated. "May I help?"

"I don't think Kazul would mind," Cimorene said. "But you'd better change clothes first. The library isn't very clean, I'm afraid."

Alianora looked down at her silk gown, which was embroidered heavily with silver and pearls, and giggled. Cimorene took her into the bedroom and found a plain, serviceable cleaning dress in the magic wardrobe. It took two tries before the wardrobe figured out that she wanted a dress for someone else, but once it caught on, it provided a splendid selection in Alianora's size. Then they went to the library and got to work.

Cleaning was much more enjoyable with Alianora for company. By the time they finished dusting and straightening the last bookcases, the two girls were fast friends, and Alianora was comfortable enough to ask Cimorene straight out how it was that she had come to volunteer for a dragon.

"It's a long story," Cimorene said, but Alianora insisted on hearing it. So Cimorene told her and then asked how Alianora had happened to be carried off by Woraug.

To her surprise, Alianora flushed. "I think it was the only thing left that they could think of," she said, not very clearly. "My family, I mean."

"I don't understand," Cimorene said.

"It's because I'm not a very satisfactory princess," Alianora said. "I *tried*, I really did, but. . . . It started when the wicked fairy came to my christening."

"She put a curse on you?"

"*No.* She ate cake and ice cream until she nearly burst and danced with my Uncle Arthur until two in the morning and had a *wonderful* time. So she went home without cursing me, and Aunt Ermintrude says that that's where the whole problem started."

"Lots of princesses don't have christening curses," said Cimorene.

"Not if a wicked fairy comes to the christening," Alianora said positively. "And that was only the beginning. When I turned sixteen, Aunt Ermintrude sent me a gold spinning wheel for my birthday, and I sat down and spun. I didn't prick my finger or *anything*."

Cimorene was beginning to see what Alianora

was getting at. "Well, if you didn't have a christening curse . . ."

"So Aunt Ermintrude told Mama to put me and a spinning wheel in a room full of straw and have me spin it into gold," Alianora went on. "And I tried! But all I could manage was linen thread, and whoever heard of a princess who can spin straw into linen thread?"

"It's a little unusual, certainly."

"Then they gave me a loaf of bread and told me to walk through the forest and give some to anyone who asked. I did *exactly* what they told me, and the second beggar-woman was a fairy in disguise, but instead of saying that whenever I spoke, diamonds and roses would drop from my mouth, she said that since I was so kind, I would never have any problems with my teeth."

"Really? Did it work?"

"Well, I haven't had a toothache since I met her."

"I'd much rather have good teeth than have diamonds and roses drop out of my mouth whenever I said something," Cimorene said. "Think how uncomfortable it would be if you accidentally talked in your sleep! You'd wake up rolling around on thorns and rocks."

"That never occurred to me," Alianora said, much struck.

"Was that everything?" Cimorene asked.

"No," Alianora said. "Aunt Ermintrude persuaded one of her fairy friends to give me a gown and a pair of glass slippers to go to a ball in the next kingdom over. And I *broke* one before I even got out of the castle!"

"That's not so surprising," Cimorene said. "Glass slippers are for deserving merchants' daughters, not for princesses."

"Try telling Aunt Ermintrude that," Alianora said. "I think she was the one who found out that Woraug was going to ravage a village just over the border and arranged for me to go and visit on the right day so I could be carried off. She didn't even warn me. I suppose she thought that if I knew, I'd mess it up somehow."

"I don't think I would get along very well with your Aunt Ermintrude," Cimorene commented thoughtfully.

"Oh, it wasn't so bad, at least at first," Alianora said. "Woraug ignored me most of the time, especially after he found out I can't cook, and it was a real relief not to have Aunt Ermintrude around any more. Only then Gornul brought Keredwel and Zareth brought Hallanna, and . . ."

"And they've been making life miserable for you ever since," Cimorene finished. "Why don't you stand up to them?"

"I tried, but you don't know what they're like," Alianora said, sighing. "Keredwel goes on and on about correct behavior, and Hallanna dissolves in tears as soon as it looks like she's losing an argument. And they've both had *dozens* of knights and princes try to rescue them. I've only had two."

"How do you do it?" Cimorene asked. "I've had nine already, and they're a dreadful nuisance." Alianora stared at Cimorene, then began to giggle. "What's so funny?" Cimorene demanded.

"Keredwel bragged for a week because two knights and a prince tried to rescue her the first month she was here," Alianora explained between giggles. "She said it was some kind of record. You've barely been with Kazul for four weeks, and you've had *nine*, and you didn't even mention it when Keredwel was here. She's going to be furious when she finds out."

"If she wants them, she can have them," Cimorene said. Her expression grew thoughtful. "Maybe they'd be easier to get rid of if I sent them along to another princess, instead of just trying to get them to go home."

"Oh!" said Alianora, and went off into gales of laughter again. Cimorene gave her a questioning look. "It's the idea of Keredwel being –

oh, my – being rescued by a second-hand knight," Alianora gasped. "Oh, dear!"

Cimorene's eyes began to dance. "I could take a good look at them first, to make sure they're worthy of her before I sent them on," she suggested.

This was too much for either of them, and they both collapsed in laughter. "You wouldn't, really, would you?" Alianora said when she began to recover.

"Send the knights to rescue someone else? I certainly would," Cimorene said emphatically. "I meant it when I said they were a nuisance. I wouldn't want to upset Keredwel, though. I'll have to think about the best way of handling it. It's a good thing there probably won't be any more of them for a few weeks. I should have plenty of time to figure something out."

"How do you know that?" Alianora asked. Cimorene explained about the sign and Therandil and her "sprained ankle." Alianora was impressed and promised to help if she could. "I'll tell Hallanna that you've twisted your ankle. I *know* she'll tell the next knight who comes to rescue her, and then it won't matter if your Prince Therandil doesn't tell anybody."

This settled, the two girls sat down and began looking through the books and scrolls Cimorene had piled on the table. Alianora, having been brought up as a proper princess despite the tiny size of her country, did not read Latin, so Cimorene had to examine those scrolls herself. There was a sizable stack of books left, however, and Alianora waded into them with a will. It was Cimorene, however, who finally found the spell they were searching for.

"I think this is it!" she said, looking up from an ancient, crumpled scroll. " 'Being a Spell for the Resisting of Heat and Flames of All Kinds, in Particular Those Which Are the Product of Magical Beasts,' " she read. "Yes, there's a list and it includes dragons."

"I would think dragons would be at the top," Alianora said. "Is it difficult?"

"It doesn't look hard," Cimorene said, studying the page. "Some of the ingredients are pretty rare, but it says you only need them for the initial casting. After that, you can reactivate the spell just by throwing a pinch of dried feverfew in the air and reciting a couplet."

"That's not bad," Alianora said. She came around the table and peered over Cimorene's shoulder at the faded ink. "Is it Latin?"

"No, it's just an ornate style of writing," Cimorene assured her. "It's not hard to read, once you get the hang of it. See, there's the couplet.

''Power of water, wind and earth,
Turn the fire back to its birth.''

"It's a variation on a dragon spell," Cimorene added thoughtfully.

"How do you know that?" Alianora asked.

"The court wizard at home mentioned it when he was teaching me magic," Cimorene replied, studying the directions.

"Then maybe it really *will* work on dragon fire. Can we get all the ingredients for the initial casting?"

"I think so, but it'll take a while," Cimorene said. "I don't have any wolfsbane, and I'm not at all sure about unicorn water. Come on, let's check and see what we need to get."

They took the scroll into the kitchen and began hunting through the shelves and supplies. They found more of the ingredients than Cimorene had expected, and she began to wonder whether one of Kazul's previous princesses might have studied magic. They did not, however, find any wolfsbane or unicorn water, nor were they able to locate any white eagle feathers. Alianora discovered a very cobwebby jar labeled "Powdered Hens' Teeth," but it was quite empty.

Cimorene made a list of the ingredients they still needed, while Alianora changed back into her pearl-embroidered dress. Alianora took a copy of the list and went back to her quarters, much excited, to see whether she happened to have anything useful in the dusty, disused corners of her dragon's kitchen. Cimorene doubted that she would find anything, but there was no harm in letting her look.

As soon as Alianora left, Cimorene tidied up the kitchen and put all but two of the books back on the shelves in the library. One was the scroll of spells in which she had found the fireproofing spell, because she wanted to take a more careful look at some of the other charms and enchantments it described. The other book was a fat volume bound in worn leather, with the words *Historia Draconum* in cracked and flaking gold leaf on the cover. Cimorene had decided it was time she really got to work on her Latin.

CHAPTER 6

In Which the Wizards Do Some Snooping, and Cimorene Snoops Back

For the next three weeks, Cimorene spent most of her free time studying the fire-proofing spell and collecting the ingredients she would need to cast it. A few, like the wolfsbane and feverfew, she could gather herself from the herbs that grew on the slopes of the mountains. Alianora found a little jar of hippopotamus oil among the cosmetics left by her predecessor. The unicorn water Cimorene got from Morwen, after promising her a copy of the spell if it worked. She went to Kazul about the white eagle feathers, though she was a little afraid to explain what she wanted them for. She didn't want Kazul to think that she was worried about

Kazul losing her temper and accidentally roasting her. Fortunately, the dragon found the whole idea very interesting.

"It could be useful," Kazul said. "There are enough hot-tempered youngsters around that it would be well worth fireproofing the princesses who have to deal with them."

"I'm not sure I'll be able to fireproof anyone at all," Cimorene said. "I still need the white eagle feathers and the powdered hens' teeth, and nobody seems to have any."

"I'll see what I can do," Kazul said, and a few days later she dropped a bundle of white feathers at the door of the kitchen. Half a feather was stuck to one of her right claws, and another was caught between two of her teeth, and she looked very pleased with herself. Cimorene decided not to ask any awkward questions. Even Kazul, however, could not find any hens' teeth, so Cimorene had to keep putting off trying out the spell.

When she wasn't working on collecting the ingredients for the fireproofing spell, Cimorene read the *Historia Draconum*. It was very difficult at first. After all, it had been a *long* time since her last Latin lesson. She kept working at it until she started to remember the right endings for the declensions and conjugations and cases. Shortly after that she realized that she was not having to look up quite as many words as she had at the beginning.

From then on, her progress was rapid. It helped that she found the book fascinating. Dragon history was not a subject commonly taught to princesses in Linderwall. But as she was now a dragon's princess, she had personal reasons to be interested. Besides, the history of the dragons was very exciting. Every page was full of descriptions of dragons ravaging villages, carrying off princesses, defeating knights and princes (and occasionally being defeated by them), and fighting with wizards, giants, and each other. When the book wasn't describing battles, it was describing famous dragons' hoards and peculiar draconian customs.

Cimorene was in the library with the *Historia Draconum* in front of her and her Latin dictionary on the table beside her left hand when she heard someone calling from the front of the cave. She had hoped it would be at least a little longer before the knights started coming back, so she couldn't help sighing as she stuck a leather bookmark in the book and closed it. Then she went out to argue with whoever it was until they went away.

Two wizards were standing just outside the mouth of the cave. Cimorene saw their wooden staffs first, before she was close enough to see their faces. As she came nearer, she recognized the one on the left as Zemenar. The one on the right was taller and younger; his brown hair and beard showed no trace of gray. His blue and brown robes were identical to the older wizard's, except for the colors. His eyes were the same bright black as his companion's, and he looked at Cimorene in a way that made her feel uneasy.

"Good morning to you, Princess Cimorene," Zemenar said. "I thought I would take you up on your kind invitation to visit. I hope we haven't come at an inconvenient time?"

"Not at all," Cimorene said, thinking hard. She had promised Kazul that she would try to find out what Zemenar was after if he showed up, and here he was. Maybe if she convinced him that she was as silly as her sisters, he would be careless enough to let something slip.

"I thought perhaps we might have since it took you so long to come out," Zemenar said mildly, but Cimorene thought there was a hint of suspicion in his eyes.

"I must not have heard you right away," Cimorene said, batting her eyes innocently, the way her next youngest sister did whenever she had done something particularly foolish. "Kazul has quite a large set of caves, and I was in one of the ones at the back. I'm *so* sorry."

"Ah." Zemenar stroked his beard with his left

hand. "That would make it difficult for you. Perhaps we could set up a spell for you, one that would let you know whenever anyone comes to visit. It would be more pleasant for visitors, too, if they didn't have to shout. What do you think, Antorell?"

"Like the one at the headquarters of the society," the second wizard said, nodding. "We could do it in two or three minutes, right from here. It'd be easy."

Zemenar shot a dark look at his companion. Cimorene was sure that he'd wanted to pretend he was inventing a new spell, so that he would have an excuse to wander around Kazul's caves. "Quite," said Zemenar. "Well, Princess?"

"Oh, dear, I don't know," Cimorene said, doing her best to imitate the way her eldest sister behaved whenever anyone wanted her to decide anything. "It sounds very nice, but Kazul is so *picky* about where things go and how things are done. . . . No, I couldn't, I simply *couldn't* let you do anything like that without asking Kazul first."

"What a pity," Zemenar said. His companion coughed and shuffled his feet. "Ah, yes. Allow me to present my son, Antorell. I hope you don't mind my bringing him along?"

"Of course not," Cimorene said politely.

"I am pleased to make the acquaintance of

such a lovely princess," Antorell said, bowing.

Cimorene blinked. This wasn't getting any-where. Maybe if she brought them inside they'd relax a little. "Thank you," she said to Antorell. "Won't you come in and have some tea?"

"We would be delighted," Zemenar said quickly. "If you'll lead the way, Princess?"

"This way," Cimorene said. She stopped just inside the mouth of the cave and gave the wizards her sweetest and most innocent smile. "You can leave your staffs right here. Just lean them up against the wall."

Antorell looked considerably startled, and Zemenar frowned. "Is this, too, something your dragon requires?" he said.

"I don't know," Cimorene said, wrinkling her forehead the way her third-from-eldest sister did when she was puzzled (which was often). "But they'll be so awkward in the kitchen. Don't you think so? There's not much room."

"We'll manage," Zemenar said.

Cimorene hadn't really expected to get the wizards to let go of their staffs, but it had been worth a try. She shrugged and smiled and led them on into the kitchen, where she made a point of bumping into the staffs or tripping over them every time she went by. Finally Antorell turned his sideways and stuck it under the table. Zemenar hung onto his with a kind of grim, suspicious stubbornness that made Cimorene wonder whether she was fooling him at all with her pretended silliness.

The wizards made uncomfortable conversation about the weather and size of the kitchen for several minutes while Cimorene fixed the tea and poured it. "Are the rest of Kazul's caves this large?" Zemenar asked as Cimorene handed him his teacup. She had given him the one with the broken handle, even though he was a guest, because she didn't trust him.

"Oh, yes," Cimorene said. She was beginning to think she was never going to find out anything. The two wizards seemed perfectly happy to sit at the kitchen table and talk about nothing whatever for hours.

"Remarkable," said Antorell in an admiring tone. "You know, we wizards don't often get to see the inside of a dragon's cave."

I'll bet you don't, thought Cimorene as she gave him a puzzled smile. "That's too bad," she said aloud.

"Yes, it is," Zemenar said. "Perhaps you'd be willing to show us around?"

Cimorene thought very rapidly. It was obvious that she wasn't going to learn anything if the wizards just sat at the kitchen table and drank tea, so she decided to take a chance. "Well," she said in a doubtful tone, "I suppose it would be all right as long as I don't take you into the treasure rooms."

"That's fine," Antorell said, a little too quickly.

"You won't touch anything, will you?" Cimorene said as they stood up. "Kazul is *so* particular about where things are kept . . ."

"Of course not," Zemenar said, smiling insincerely.

Cimorene smiled back and led the way out into the hall. She watched the wizards carefully as she took them through the large main cave, the general storage caverns, and the big cavern where Kazul visited with other dragons. Zemenar made polite noises about the size and comfort of everything, but neither he nor Antorell seemed very interested. "And this is the library," Cimorene said, throwing the door open.

"I am impressed," Zemenar said, and Cimorene could tell that this time he meant it. She stepped sideways, so that she could keep an eye on both of the wizards at the same time.

"A remarkable collection," Antorell commented. He began walking around the room, admiring the bookshelves and scanning the titles of the books.

"What's this?" Zemenar said, bending over the table. "The *Historia Draconum*? A surprising choice for light reading, Princess." His eyes met Cimorene's, and they were hard and suspicious.

"Oh, I'm not *reading* it," Cimorene said hastily, opening her eyes very wide. "I just thought it would make the library look nicer to have a book or two sitting out on the table. More – more lived-in."

Zemenar nodded, looking relieved and faintly contemptuous. "I think it works very well, Princess," he said. "Very well indeed." Then he looked over at the other side of the room and said sharply, "Antorell! What are you doing?"

Cimorene turned her head in time to see Antorell put out a hand and deliberately tip several books off one of the shelves. "Stop that!" she said, forgetting to sound silly.

"I'm very sorry, Princess," Antorell said. "Will you help me put them back where they belong?"

Cimorene had no choice but to go over and help him. It took several minutes to get everything back in place because Antorell kept dropping things. Cimorene got quite annoyed with him and finally did it all herself. As she started to turn back to the center of the room, she caught a glimpse of Zemenar hastily closing the *Historia Draconum*. Cimorene pretended not to notice, but she made a mental note that he had been looking at something near the middle of the book.

"That was dreadfully careless of you,"

Cimorene said, frowning at Antorell.

"Very clumsy," Zemenar agreed.

"I don't know what Kazul will say when she finds out about it," Cimorene went on. "Really, it is *too* bad of you. I did ask you not to touch anything, you know."

"Yes, you did," Zemenar said. "And I wouldn't like to think that we had got you into trouble. Perhaps it would be best if you didn't mention to Kazul that we were here at all."

"I suppose I could do that," Cimorene said in a doubtful tone.

"Of course you can," Antorell said encouragingly. "And I'll come back in a few days, to make sure everything's all right."

"I think it's time we were on our way," Zemenar said, giving his son a dark look. "Thank you for showing us around, Princess."

Cimorene escorted them out of the cave and made sure they had left, then hurried back to the library. She spent the next several hours poring over the middle parts of the *Historia Draconum*, trying to figure out what Zemenar had been looking at. She was still there when Kazul arrived home and called for her.

"That wizard Zemenar finally came, and he brought his son along with him," Cimorene said as she came out of the library.

"I know," said Kazul. Her voice sounded a little thick, as if she had a cold. "I could smell them the minute I came in."

"Is that why you sound so odd?" Cimorene asked. "You're not going to sneeze, are you?"

"I don't think so," Kazul replied. "Don't worry. I'll have plenty of time to turn my head away."

"I *wish* I could get hold of some hens' teeth," Cimorene said. "That fireproofing spell—"

"Have you looked in the treasure rooms?" Kazul asked.

"No," Cimorene replied, startled. She remembered seeing a number of jars and bottles of various shapes and sizes when she had been organizing the treasure, and none of them had been labeled. "I didn't think of it, and besides, it's your treasure."

"You're my princess, at least until someone rescues you or I decide otherwise," Kazul pointed out. "Go ahead and look, and if you find any hens' teeth, use them. Be careful when you're checking the jars, though. There are one or two with lead stoppers that shouldn't be opened."

"Lead stoppers," Cimorene said. "I'll remember."

"Good. Now, what did those wizards want?"

"I'm not sure." Cimorene explained everything that had happened, including how she had seen Zemenar closing the history book as she turned and how the two wizards had been perfectly willing to leave right after that. "But just before they disappeared, Antorell said he might come back another time," Cimorene concluded. "So I don't know whether they found what they were looking for or not."

"Do you know which part of the *Historia Draconum* Zemenar was reading?" Kazul asked.

"Somewhere in the middle, a little past my bookmark," Cimorene replied. "I was just looking at it when you came in. It's the part about how the dragons came to the Mountains of Morning and settled into the caves and chose a king."

"That's the section where the *Historia* describes the Caves of Fire and Night, isn't it?" Kazul said.

Cimorene nodded. "There was a whole page about somebody finding a stone in the caves so that the dragons could pick a king. It didn't make much sense to me."

"Colin's Stone," Kazul said, nodding. "We've used it to choose our king ever since. When a king dies, all the dragons go to the Ford of Whispering Snakes in the Enchanted Forest and take turns trying to move Colin's Stone from there to the Vanishing Mountain. The one that succeeds is the next king."

"What if there are *two* dragons strong enough to move it?" Cimorene asked curiously.

"It's not a matter of strength," Kazul said. "Colin's Stone isn't much larger than you are. Even a small dragon could carry that much weight twice around the Enchanted Forest without any trouble at all. But Colin's Stone has an aura, a kind of vibration. When you carry it, you can feel it humming through your claws, and the humming gets stronger the farther you go until your bones are shaking. Most dragons have to drop it or be shaken to pieces, but there's always one who is . . . suited to the stone. For that dragon, the stone's humming is just a pleasant buzz, so of course it's easy to get it to the Vanishing Mountain."

"You sound as if you've had experience," Cimorene said.

"Of course," Kazul responded matter-of-factly. "I was old enough to participate in the tests when the last king died." She smiled reminiscently. "I got farther than anyone expected me to, though I wasn't one of the top ten by any means."

Cimorene tilted her head to one side, considering. "I think I'm glad you didn't win."

"Oh? Why is that?" Kazul sounded amused.

"Because you wouldn't have had any use for a princess if you were the Queen of the Dragons, and if you hadn't decided to take me on, that yellow-green dragon Moranz would probably have eaten me," Cimorene explained.

"You mean, if I were the King of the Dragons," Kazul corrected her. "Queen of the Dragons is a dull job."

"But you're a female!" Cimorene said. "If you'd carried Colin's Stone from the Ford of Whispering Snakes to the Vanishing Mountain, you'd have had to be a queen, wouldn't you?"

"No, of course not," Kazul said. "Queen of the Dragons is a totally different job from King, and it's not one I'm particularly interested in. Most people aren't. I think the position's been vacant since Oraun tore his wing and had to retire."

"But King Tokoz is a male dragon!" Cimorene said, then frowned. "Isn't he?"

"Yes, yes, but that has nothing to do with it," Kazul said a little testily. " 'King' is the name of the job. It doesn't matter who holds it."

Cimorene stopped and thought for a moment. "You mean that dragons don't care whether their king is male or female; the title is the same no matter who the ruler is."

"That's right. We like to keep things simple."

"Oh." Cimorene decided to return to the original topic of conversation before the dragon's "simple" ideas confused her any further. "Why would the wizards be interested in Colin's

Stone if it's only used for picking out the kings of the dragons?"

"I doubt that they are," Kazul replied. "However, Colin's Stone was found in the Caves of Fire and Night, and wizards have always been interested in the caves. But the dragons control most of them, and all the easy entrances are ours, so the wizards have never been able to find out as much as they would like. The *Historia Draconum* is one of the few books that talks about the caves at all, and there aren't many copies. I'll wager Zemenar would have stolen it outright if he'd thought he could get away with it."

"I thought the dragons let wizards into the Caves of Fire and Night," Cimorene objected. "Why would Zemenar be poking through history books looking for information if he can go and look at them whenever he wants to?"

"We don't let wizards visit the caves whenever they want," Kazul said. "If we did, they'd be running in and out all the time, and nobody would be able to breathe without sneezing. No, they're limited to certain days and times, and if they want to visit the Caves of Fire and Night otherwise, they have to use one of the entrances we don't control. Few of them try. The other ways of getting into the caves are very dangerous, even for wizards."

"Maybe they're looking for an easier way in."

"Mmm." Kazul did not seem to be paying much attention. She thought for a moment, then turned toward the cave mouth. "I'm going to go see Gaurim. Roxim said a book had been stolen from her library, and I want to know which one. I'll be back in a few hours."

"I think I'll go look at the *Historia Draconum* again while you're gone," Cimorene said thoughtfully. "If there *is* something useful in it about the Caves of Fire and Night, maybe I can find it, now that I know what I'm looking for."

Cimorene spent the rest of the afternoon carefully translating the chapter that talked about the caves. She was disappointed to find that there was very little about the caves themselves, though what was there was interesting. The book told how the dragons had discovered the back way into the caves and described some of the things they had found in them – caverns full of blue and green fire, pools of black liquid that would cast a cloud of darkness for twenty miles around if you poured three drops on the ground, walls made of crystal that multiplied every sound a thousandfold, rocks that spurted fire when they were broken. Most of the rest of the chapter was about Colin's Stone, and how it was found and taken out of the caves by the first

King of the Dragons.

Kazul returned just before dinner, and she and Cimorene compared notes. Cimorene told Kazul what she had learned from the chapter on the Caves of Fire and Night, and then Kazul explained what she had learned from Gaurim.

"The stolen book was *The Kings of the Dragons*, and the entire first section was about Colin's Stone and the Caves of Fire and Night," Kazul said. "And only a wizard could have got past the spells and safeguards Gaurim puts on her library. I think that settles it. The wizards are definitely collecting information about the Caves of Fire and Night."

"Then why do they keep looking at books of dragon history?" Cimorene asked. "It seems like a roundabout way of finding out whatever it is that they want to know."

"There isn't any other way to do it," Kazul said. "Nobody but dragons has ever had much to do with the caves, and no one has written much about them except in dragon histories. Even the wizards weren't particularly interested in them until a few years ago, except as a reliable route into the Enchanted Forest."

"But from what I've been reading in the *Historia Draconum*, the caves sound fascinating," Cimorene said. "You mean to say that *no one* has ever written anything about the Caves of Fire and Night except dragons?"

"That's—" Kazul stopped suddenly, and her eyes narrowed. "No, that's *not* right. There was a rather rumpled scholar who talked his way into the caves a century or so back, and after he left he wrote an extremely dry book about what he found there. I'd forgotten about him."

"Do you have a copy?" Cimorene asked hopefully.

"No," Kazul said. "But I don't think the Society of Wizards does, either. There weren't very many of them printed, and a lot of those were lost in a flood a few years later. Some hero or other shoved a giant into a lake to drown him. The silly clunch didn't realize that if he put something that big into a lake, the water would have to go *somewhere*."

"Well, that doesn't do us much good," Cimorene said. "It's nice that the Society of Wizards doesn't have a copy of that book, but if we can't get hold of one either—"

"I didn't say that," Kazul said. "I don't have a copy myself, but I know who does."

"Who?" Cimorene said impatiently.

"Morwen. I'm afraid you're not going to be able to work on that fireproofing spell of yours tomorrow. We're going to take a trip to the Enchanted Forest instead."

CHAPTER 7

*In Which Cimorene and Kazul
Make a Journey Underground*

Cimorene was surprised that Kazul intended
to take her to visit Morwen, and she was
not entirely sure she liked the idea. She had
heard a great deal about the Enchanted Forest,
and none of it was reassuring. People who
traveled there were always getting changed into
flowers or trees or animals or rocks, or doing
something careless and having their heads
turned backward, or being carried off by ogres
or giants or trolls, or enchanted by witches or
wicked fairies. It did not sound like a place for a
casual, pleasant visit.

On the other hand, it seemed unlikely that
anything dreadful would happen to Cimorene

if she were traveling with a dragon, and she was looking forward to seeing Morwen again. Besides, Cimorene was curious.

"And anyway," she said to herself, "Kazul says I'm going, and there's no point in worrying about it if I don't have any choice." Nevertheless, she decided to take one of the smaller magic swords along with her, if Kazul said it was all right. Cimorene saw no point in taking unnecessary chances.

Kazul had no objection, so Cimorene picked out a small, plain-looking sword in a worn leather scabbard that made the wearer invincible, and they started off. Cimorene had assumed that Kazul would fly through the pass, but Kazul said no.

"It's not that easy to get into the Enchanted Forest," she explained. "At least, not if you're trying to get in. Princes and youngest sons and particularly clever tailors stumble into it by accident all the time, but if one wants to go there on purpose, one has to follow the proper route."

"I didn't think dragons had that kind of problem," Cimorene said.

"Dragons don't," Kazul replied. "But you're not a dragon."

So instead of flying through the Pass of Silver Ice, Kazul led Cimorene through the tunnels.

Cimorene had to walk very quickly to keep up, even though Kazul was moving slowly. It was not long before she was wishing that the tunnels were high enough for her to ride on Kazul's back. The route twisted around and up and back and forth and down and around again until Cimorene was thoroughly lost. Finally they came to a gate made of iron bars that completely blocked the passage. Cimorene studied it carefully, but she could see no sign of a handle or a lock.

"This is the entrance to the Caves of Fire and Night," Kazul said. "Be careful from here on, and don't wander away or you'll get lost."

Cimorene refrained from saying that as far as she was concerned, they were lost already. "How are you going to open it?" she asked instead.

"Like this," said Kazul.

> *"By night and flame and shining rock*
> *Open thou thy hidden lock.*
> *Alberolingarn!"*

As the sound of Kazul's voice died away, the iron gate swung silently open. "That's a very unusual opening spell," Cimorene commented, impressed.

"It wasn't always that complicated," Kazul said. She sounded almost apologetic. "I believe the first version was very simple, just 'Open sesame,' but word got around and we had to change it."

Cimorene nodded and followed Kazul through the gate and into the Caves of Fire and Night. For the first hundred yards or so, the only difference Cimorene could see between these caves and the ordinary tunnels on the other side of the gate was that the Caves of Fire and Night were warmer. Then, very suddenly, her lamp went out, plunging everything into complete and utter blackness.

Cimorene stopped walking immediately. "Kazul?"

"It's quite all right, Princess," Kazul's disembodied voice said from out of the darkness. "This happens all the time here. Don't bother trying to relight the lamp. Just put your hand on my elbow and follow along that way."

"All right," Cimorene said doubtfully. She groped with her free hand in the direction of Kazul's voice and scraped her knuckles on the dragon's scales. "Ow!"

"Take your time," Kazul advised.

"I'm ready," Cimorene said. Her right hand was pressed flat against the cool, rough-edged scales at the back of Kazul's left forearm. "Just don't move too fast, or I'll lose you or get stepped on or something."

Kazul did her best to oblige, but Cimorene still had difficulty in keeping up. She had to take at least three steps for every one of Kazul's, and it seemed that every time she moved her foot, she hit a rock or an uneven place in the tunnel floor. Then she would stumble, and her hand would scrape and slide against Kazul's scales, so that she was afraid she would lose contact with the dragon.

"Are you sure I shouldn't try and relight the lamp?" Cimorene asked after her fifth painful stumble-and-slide.

"Quite sure," Kazul said. "You see, it isn't — ah, there it goes." While Kazul was speaking, there was a flicker of light, and then the darkness rolled aside like a curtain being pulled. Cimorene found herself standing in a large cave whose walls glittered as if they were studded with thousands of tiny mirrors. The lamp in her left hand was burning cheerfully once more.

"*Was* it the lamp?" Cimorene asked after studying it for a moment. "Or was it me?"

"It was the caves," Kazul said. "That was one of the reasons they're 'of night' as well as 'of fire.'"

"Only *one* of the reasons?" Cimorene said thoughtfully. "I don't like the sound of that."

"You'll be quite all right as long as you're with me," Kazul assured her. "Very few things are willing to mess with a dragon, even in the dark. And the periods of darkness don't last long. It's because the magic of these caves doesn't affect us as much as other people, or so I'm told."

"You mean that blackness is likely to come back?"

Kazul nodded.

"Then let's get as far as we can before it does," Cimorene said, and started across the cave.

There were four tunnels leading out of the opposite side of the glittering cavern. Kazul took the second from the left without hesitating an instant.

"Where do all these tunnels go?" Cimorene asked, glancing at the other three openings as she followed Kazul.

"The one on the right end leads to a chain of caverns," Kazul said over her shoulder. "The first few are quite ordinary, but then you come to one full of hot sulphur pools. Some of the older dragons bathe there. They claim the water is good for rheumatism. Beyond that is a cave with molten silver dripping down the walls, and the chain ends at a deep chasm with a river of red-hot melted rock at the bottom."

"Doesn't sound very attractive," Cimorene commented.

"The dwarfsmiths find it very useful for forging magic swords," Kazul assured her. "The second tunnel on the right takes you into a maze. The tunnels and caverns constantly shift around, so that no matter how carefully you mark your way, you always get lost."

"Even dragons?"

Kazul nodded. "Though I believe there was one prince who managed to find his way out with a magic ball of string."

"Oh, bother!" said Cimorene. The lights had gone out again, just as they emerged into a small cave.

"It's quite all right. This part's easy," Kazul said.

"Next time I'm going to bring a cane," Cimorene muttered. "Where do the other tunnels lead?"

"The one on the far left goes through a couple of caverns that are pretty, but not very interesting. We're always chasing knights and princes out of it, though. They come for flasks of water from the bottomless pool at the far end."

"What does it do?" Cimorene asked. "Ow!" She had just banged her right elbow against the wall of the cave in the dark.

"It casts a cloud of darkness for twenty miles around when it's poured on the ground," Kazul replied.

"How useful," Cimorene muttered balefully, rubbing her elbow.

"And this tunnel leads to the Enchanted Forest, by way of the King's Cave," Kazul finished.

"Oh, good. I was hoping to see that," Cimorene said. The King's Cave was the chamber where the first King of the Dragons had found Colin's Stone, and the *Historia Draconum* had not described it anywhere near well enough to suit Cimorene. "And here's the light coming back, thank goodness. Let's hurry before it goes again."

They went through three small caves and two more periods of blackness before they reached the King's Cave. Kazul pointed out various locations of interest, such as the wall of crystal with a chip in one corner where the Prince of the Ruby Throne had stolen a piece to make a magic ring and the jewel-studded cavern where the King of the Dragons met with people who needed impressing. There was one very eerie cave full of slabs of black rock. Most were standing on end, though a few had fallen over. Kazul said they were all enchanted princes.

"All of them?" Cimorene asked, appalled. There were at least forty of the stone slabs, and the cave was quite crowded.

Kazul shook her head. "No, the one on the end there is just an ordinary boulder."

"How did it happen?"

"The princes came to steal some of the Water of Healing from the well at the end of the cave," Kazul said. "There are two dippers by the well: one is tin, the other is solid gold and covered with jewels. The princes all tried to use the gold one, even though they'd been told that only the tin dipper would work. It's no more than they deserve."

Cimorene frowned, thinking of some of the princes she had known. "Well, I won't deny that they probably behaved foolishly, but—"

"Foolishly!" Kazul snorted. "Any reasonably well-educated prince ought to have sense enough to follow directions when he's on a quest, but all of these fellows were sure they knew better. If they'd simply done what they were told, they wouldn't be here."

"Still, turning them into slabs of stone forever seems a little extreme."

"Oh, they won't be stone forever," Kazul said. "Sooner or later someone will come along who has the sense not to improvise, and he'll succeed in getting the water. Then he'll use some of it to disenchant this lot, and the cave will be empty for a while until the next batch of young idiots starts arriving."

Cimorene felt better knowing that the princes would someday be freed, though she had sense enough not to try doing it herself. Since she had not been sent on a quest for the Water of Healing, it was highly unlikely that she would be able to disenchant the princes even if she succeeded in taking the water. And she knew enough about quests and enchantments and the obtaining of things with magical properties to know that she would probably get into a lot of trouble if she tried. So she tucked the matter into the back of her mind and followed Kazul through the stone-filled cavern. She was careful not to step on any of the fallen slabs.

Just outside the entrance to the next cave, Kazul stopped. "This," she said, "is the King's Cave. We have to cross it as quickly as we can. Don't stop in the middle, and don't say anything while we're inside. Understand? Good. Come on, then."

As soon as she stepped inside the cave, Cimorene understood the reason for Kazul's request for silence. The walls, the ceiling, and the floor were made of dark, shiny stone that multiplied and threw back echoes of even the smallest sound. The soft scraping of Kazul's scales against the floor sounded like thirty men sawing wood, and the tiny gasp Cimorene gave at the sight and sound of the cave was as loud as if she had shouted. Cimorene went on as quickly and carefully as she could.

Halfway across, she noticed the vibration. It

began as a gentle and not unpleasant buzzing in her bones, unrelated to the loud and continually multiplying echoes of her passage, though it, too, grew stronger the farther into the cave she went. Kazul was in front of her now, and she saw the dragon's tail lash once, as if in pain or anger. Suddenly she remembered Kazul's description of the aura that made it impossible for most dragons to carry Colin's Stone, and that this was the place where Colin's Stone had been found. No wonder Kazul was uncomfortable.

Cimorene found herself wishing she could stop and pay attention to the humming in her bones, but she remembered Kazul's directions and continued walking. She had nearly reached the exit when she saw a pebble about the size of her thumbnail, made of the same dark, shiny stone as the cavern walls. Kazul had said nothing about picking things up, so Cimorene veered a little to the right and scooped the pebble up as she passed. A moment later she was out of the cave.

"Phew!" said Kazul. "I'm glad that's over. From here on, it should be easy."

"Good," said Cimorene. She dropped the pebble into her pocket to look at more closely later and followed Kazul down the narrow, winding tunnel.

CHAPTER 8

*In Which Cimorene and Kazul Pay a Call,
and Cimorene Gets into a Fight*

A few minutes later they came out of the
Caves of Fire and Night into bright sunlight. Cimorene had to shade her eyes against
the sudden glare. As her eyes adjusted, she saw
a large clearing around the mouth of the cave.
The ground was covered with short grass, so
lush and dense that it made Cimorene think of
green fur. Here and there a tiny flower twinkled
among the blades of grass. At the edge of the
clearing the forest began, but Cimorene could
only make out the first row of trees. They were
enormous, so large that they dwarfed even
Kazul.

"Leave the lamp here," Kazul said. "There's

no sense in carting it around the forest when we won't need it until we come back."

Cimorene set the lamp on the ground just inside the mouth of the cave. "Now what?" she said.

"Now we go to Morwen's," Kazul said. "And we'll get there more quickly if you ride. If you climb up on that rock over there, you ought to be able to get on my back without too much trouble."

"Are you sure you don't mind?" Cimorene said, scrambling up onto the rock Kazul had indicated.

"I wouldn't have suggested it if I minded," Kazul said. "Right there will be fine. You can hang onto the spike in front of you and you won't foul my wings if I have to take off suddenly."

Cimorene did not like the implication that there were things in the Enchanted Forest that were nasty enough to make a dragon want to take off suddenly, but she did not say so. It was too late to back out, and she certainly wasn't going to wait at the mouth of the cave all alone while Kazul went off to visit Morwen. There was no reason to think that waiting would be any safer than going along.

As soon as Cimorene was settled, Kazul set off into the forest at a rapid pace. At first Cimorene had to concentrate on holding on, but after a while she began to get the hang of it. Soon she was able to look at some of the things they were passing. The trees were huge; Cimorene guessed that even if there were four of her, holding hands, she would not be able to reach all the way around one of the trunks. The ground was carpeted with bright green moss that looked even thicker than the grass in the clearing. Cimorene saw no flowers in it, but she spotted several bushes and a vine with three different colors of fruit.

Kazul changed course several times for no reason that Cimorene could see, but she did not like to distract the dragon by asking questions. They passed a mansion guarded by a fence made of gold and a short tower without any windows or doors. Then Kazul splashed through a shallow stream and made a sharp turn. The trees thinned a little, and Kazul stopped in front of a neat gray house with a wide porch and a red roof. Over the door was a black-and-gold sign in large block letters reading, "NONE OF THIS NONSENSE, PLEASE!"

There were several cats of various sizes and colors perched on the porch railing or lying in the sun. As Cimorene dismounted, Kazul said to one of them, "Would you be good enough to tell Morwen that I'm here and would like to talk to her?"

The cat, a large gray tom, blinked its yellow eyes at Kazul. Then he jumped down from the porch rail and sauntered into the house, his tail held high as if to say, "I'm doing this as a particular favor, mind, and don't you forget it."

"He doesn't seem very impressed," Cimorene commented in some amusement.

"Why should he be?" Kazul said.

"Well, you're a dragon," Cimorene answered, a little taken aback.

"What difference does that make to a cat?"

Fortunately, Cimorene did not have to find an answer, for at that moment Morwen appeared in the doorway. She was wearing the same black robe she had worn when she visited Cimorene, or another one exactly like it, and she peered through her glasses with the air of someone studying an unexpected and rather peculiar puzzle.

"Good morning, Kazul," she said after a moment. "This is a surprise."

"Good," said Kazul. "If you aren't expecting us to be here, no one else is, either."

"That's the way of things, is it?" Morwen commented thoughtfully. "How much of a hurry are you in?"

"Not much of one, as long as no one knows we're here," Kazul replied.

"Then Cimorene had better get down and have something to drink," Morwen said in a tone that forbade contradiction. "There's cider, or goat's milk, though if you want that, you'll have the cats after you, or I can put a kettle on for tea. Good gracious, what have you done to your hand?"

While Morwen had been talking, Cimorene had turned and slid carefully down Kazul's side. It was a long slide, and when her feet hit the ground, she had to put out a hand to keep from falling. Morwen's exclamation made her blink in surprise, and she looked down. The palm of her right hand was covered with blood from half a dozen deep slashes and as many scrapes.

"Oh, dear," Cimorene said. "It must have happened in the caves, when it was so dark. I didn't realize. It doesn't hurt at all."

"Hurting or not, it needs attention," Morwen said firmly. "Come inside, and I'll see to it while Kazul tells me why you're here. You'll have to go around the back this time," she added, turning to Kazul. "The front steps won't take the weight. A gnome stole one of the supports, and I haven't had time to get it fixed yet. Pesky creatures – they're worse than mice."

"Don't the cats keep the mice away?" Cimorene asked, mildly puzzled.

"Yes, but they don't do a thing about gnomes, which is why gnomes are worse. Mind the step."

Kazul started walking while Morwen shooed Cimorene up the wooden steps and into the house. Several of the cats eyed Cimorene curiously as she passed, and a tortoiseshell kitten got up and followed her in.

The front door led into a large, airy room with an iron stove in one corner. There was a good deal of furniture, but everything except the table and the stove had at least one cat on top of it. Morwen frowned at a fat and fluffy Persian that was sitting on one of the chairs. The cat stood up, yawned, gave its front paws a cursory lick or two just to show that this was all his own idea, and jumped down onto the floor. As Cimorene sat down in the vacated chair, there was a knock at the wooden door on the opposite side of the room.

"That'll be Kazul," Morwen said. She crossed to the door and opened it. "Come in. I'll get you some cider as soon as I've seen to Cimorene's hand."

Morwen's back door did not seem to get any larger, and Kazul certainly did not get any smaller, but when she put her head through the doorway, her scales did not even scrape the sides. The rest of her followed with no apparent difficulty, and somehow there was plenty of room in the kitchen even after she got inside.

Kazul settled down along the far wall, where she would be out of the way, and as soon as she stopped moving, six cats jumped onto various portions of her tail, back, and shoulders. Neither Kazul nor Morwen seemed to notice. Morwen took a small tin box from a shelf beside the stove and sat down at the table beside Cimorene. "Now, tell me what you're here for," she said, taking a roll of linen and two jars of ointment out of the box. "Apart from my cider, I mean."

"Cimorene had some interesting visitors yesterday," Kazul said.

"If they were interesting, they can't have been knights," Morwen commented.

"They weren't," Kazul said. "They were wizards, and they went to a lot of trouble to get a look at my copy of the *Historia Draconum*. The part that describes the Caves of Fire and Night."

"And you think that's why they've been sniffing around the Mountains of Morning for the past six months," Morwen said. "How did you find out what they were looking at? Or did they ask permission?"

"I don't think Zemenar would ask permission for anything even if he was sure he'd get it," Cimorene said. "He'd consider it beneath him.

No, I saw him shut the book, and he was only a little further along from where I'd left my bookmark. Ow! That stings."

"Good," Morwen said. "It's supposed to." She closed the jar of salve she had been smearing on Cimorene's palm and began wrapping the injured hand in the linen bandage. "Did Zemenar get what he was after?"

"I don't think so," Cimorene said. "He said he wanted to come back for another visit, and I don't think he'd have done that if he'd found whatever he was looking for."

"That seems like a reasonable assumption," Morwen said. "Though wizards aren't always reasonable. There, that should take care of things. Don't take the bandage off for at least four days, and if you're going to cook anything that has fennel in it, stir it left-handed."

"Zemenar's interest in the *Historia Draconum* isn't the only thing that points to his curiosity about the Caves of Fire and Night," Kazul said, and explained about the book that had been stolen. "There have been other incidents as well, and nearly all the wizards we've caught poking around have been somewhere in or near the caves. That's why no one thought much about it at first. Ever since King Tokoz made that agreement with the Society of Wizards, they've been claiming they're supposed to have more time in the caves than we're willing to give them. Everyone thought this was more of the same."

"Not everyone," Morwen said, giving Kazul a sharp look.

"I am widely considered to be unduly suspicious of everyone and everything," Kazul said in a dry tone. "Particularly wizards."

"And what do your suspicions make of this business?"

"I think Zemenar is trying to find out something about the Caves of Fire and Night," Kazul said. "Something he hasn't been able to learn from visiting the caves in person, hence his recent interest in histories that describe the caves, however briefly."

"And you're hoping I have something in my library that will help you figure out what it is," Morwen concluded.

"I don't hope," Kazul said. "I know. Unless someone has run off with your copy of DeMontmorency's *A Journey Through the Caves of Fire and Night.*"

"If someone has, he'll regret it," Morwen said. "Wait here, and I'll check." She rose and went out. Through the doorway Cimorene could see a room full of tall, dark-stained shelves.

Cimorene blinked. "Isn't that the door you came in through?" she asked Kazul.

Kazul nodded. "Of course."

"I thought it led out into Morwen's yard."

"It leads wherever Morwen wants it to lead," Kazul said.

"I see," said Cimorene, wishing her father's court philosopher were there. He was very pompous and stuffy, particularly about magic, which he claimed was 90 percent trickery and the rest illusion. Cimorene had found him very trying. Dealing with Morwen's door would probably have given him a headache.

Morwen came back into the kitchen holding a thin red book. "Here it is. I'm sorry it took me so long to find it, but the non-fiction isn't organized as well as it should be yet."

Kazul surged to her feet, shedding cats in all directions. The cats gave her reproachful looks and then stalked out of the front door with affronted dignity. Kazul paid no attention. She curled her head around to peer at the book over Morwen's shoulder.

"I suppose you'll want to borrow it?" Morwen said.

"I certainly do," Kazul said. "Is there a problem?"

"Only if it gets stolen," Morwen said. "There are very few of these around and I'm not sure I could replace it."

"I'll keep it in the vault with the treasure,"

Kazul promised. "Zemenar won't think to look for it there, and even if he does, he won't get in. I've got enough anti-wizard spells on the door to stop the whole Society. They can't get in unless someone invites them."

"All right," Morwen said, handing the book to Kazul. "Is that everything you came for?"

"No," said Kazul. She looked at Morwen with limpid eyes and went on in a plaintive tone, "I still haven't had any cider."

Morwen laughed and went to one of the cupboards. She pulled out two mugs and a large mixing bowl and filled them with an amber-colored liquid she poured from a heavy-looking pottery jug. She set the mixing bowl in front of Kazul and gave one of the mugs to Cimorene, then sat down with the second mug herself.

They were in Morwen's kitchen for over an hour, drinking cider and speculating about what the wizards were up to. After a while several of the cats came back, and Morwen gave them a dish of goat's milk, which soothed their ruffled feelings somewhat.

"How is that fireproofing spell of yours coming?" Morwen asked as she returned to the table.

"I have everything I need except the powdered hens' teeth, and I'm beginning to think I'm never going to find any," Cimorene said. "Kazul has offered to let me look through the jars in the treasury, but if there isn't any there, I don't know where I'll look next."

"Really," Morwen said, giving Kazul a sharp look. "Well, if you can't find any hens' teeth, you could try substituting snake fingernails or the hair from a turtle's egg. I wouldn't try it except as a last resort, though. Altering spells is a very tricky business."

At last they had to leave. Kazul went out the same way she had come in while Cimorene watched in fascination. Then Cimorene and Morwen went onto the front porch. Kazul sidled up to the house, and Cimorene stood on the porch railing to climb onto her back. The cats were seriously affronted by this maneuver and expressed their displeasure in reproachful glances and low yowls.

"Don't take any notice," Morwen said. "It only encourages them."

Cimorene nodded. "Thank you for everything."

"You're quite welcome," Morwen answered. "Don't wait too long to come again."

"You'd better take this, Princess," Kazul said, reaching back over her shoulder to hand Morwen's book to Cimorene. "I can't carry it and run at the same time."

Cimorene took the book and tucked it into her pocket. "I'm all set," she said, and they started off.

Cimorene enjoyed the ride back to the Mountains of Morning. She was now sufficiently accustomed to riding on a dragon to be able to concentrate on looking at the forest as it flashed past. The trees seemed almost identical to one another, but Cimorene spotted quite a few odd-looking bushes and vines, and twice she thought she saw small faces staring out at her from among leafy branches.

They reached the threshold of the caves much sooner than Cimorene expected. Kazul waited while she slid to the ground, then said, "The entrance is a little narrow. I'll go first and make sure there's nothing unpleasant waiting for us."

Cimorene nodded, and Kazul vanished into the cave. Before Cimorene could follow, she heard a shrill cry above her. She looked up and saw an enormous white bird plummeting toward her, its clawed feet extended to attack. For an instant, Cimorene was frozen by surprise and fear. Then she ducked and reached for her sword.

She was almost too slow. The bird was on top of her, shrieking and slashing, before she had done more than grasp the hilt of her weapon. But the sword seemed to leap out of the scabbard as soon as she touched it, and she swung clumsily as she rolled aside. She did not expect to do any damage, just to force the bird to back away a little, but she felt the sword connect and heard a wail of pain from the bird. Thanking all her lucky stars individually and by name, Cimorene twisted and scrambled to her feet, sword ready.

There was nothing for her to guard against. The sword stroke had been more effective than she realized. The bird was dying. As she stared at it, it raised its head.

"*You* killed me?" the bird said incredulously. "But you're a *maiden*."

"Actually, she's a princess," Kazul's voice said from behind Cimorene. "*My* princess, so you'd have been in even bigger trouble if you'd succeeded in carrying her off."

"I don't think I could have done it if I hadn't had a magic sword," said Cimorene, who was beginning to wish she hadn't. She had never hurt anyone before, and she didn't like it.

"Just my luck," the bird said disgustedly. "Oh, well, fair's fair. You killed me, so you get my forfeit."

"You're not dead yet," Cimorene said. "If you'll let me near, I can try to stop the bleeding—"

"Not a chance," the bird said. It was beginning to sound rather faint. "Do you want the forfeit or don't you?"

"Take it," Kazul advised.

Cimorene said nothing, and after a moment the bird said, "All right, then. Under my left wing, you'll find three black feathers. If you drop one and wish to be somewhere else, you'll find yourself there in the twinkling of an eye. Any questions?"

"Can I take anyone else with me?" Cimorene asked, thinking that if the bird was so determined to give her the feathers, she might as well cooperate with it.

The bird looked at her with respect. "Will wonders never cease. For once a human with sense is getting the forfeit. Yes, you can take someone with you, as long as you're touching him. Same for objects; if you can carry it, you can take it with you. You get one trip per feather. That's all."

"But—" said Cimorene, and stopped. The bird's head had fallen back, and it was clearly quite dead.

"Don't feel too bad," Kazul said perceptively. "If it had succeeded in carrying you off, it would have fed you to its nestlings."

"Fed me to its nestlings?" Cimorene discovered that she had lost her sympathy for the dead bird. "What a horrid thing to do!" She hesitated. "Won't the nestlings starve, now that the bird is dead?"

"No, one of the other birds will take over the chore of feeding them for a few weeks until they're big enough to catch their own food," Kazul said. "Now, clean that sword and take your feathers, and let's get going. I want to have a look at that book of Morwen's."

Cimorene nodded and did as she was told. The three black feathers were right where the bird had said they would be, and she put them in her pocket with Morwen's book and the black pebble from the Caves of Fire and Night. She wiped the sword on the grass several times, then finished cleaning it with her handkerchief. When she finished, she left the handkerchief beside the dead bird and followed Kazul into the Caves of Fire and Night.

CHAPTER 9

In Which Therandil Is a Dreadful Nuisance, and Cimorene Casts a Spell

The rest of the trip home was uneventful. Passing through the King's Cave seemed easier going in the opposite direction, and the impenetrable darkness only descended once. As soon as they arrived, Kazul took the book Morwen had lent them and curled herself around a rock just outside the mouth of the cave to study it while Cimorene made dinner. She pored over the book all evening, and Cimorene found it fascinating to watch the dragon delicately turning pages with her claws. Early the next day Kazul went off to consult with Roxim.

Cimorene was rather stiff from all the dragon-riding she had done the previous day, so she decided not to do any more cleaning. Instead, she spent the morning in Kazul's treasure room, sorting through likely bottles and jars for those that might possibly contain powdered hens' teeth. Remembering Kazul's advice, she started by setting aside all the bottles she could find that had lead stoppers. Since the light was not very good, she took the jars and bottles that looked as if they might be worth investigating and piled them in her apron, so as to carry them outside more easily.

She had nearly finished sorting when she heard a voice calling faintly in the distance.

"Bother!" she said. "I *did* hope they'd leave me alone a *little* longer."

She bundled the last five bottles into her apron without looking at them and, not forgetting to lock the door behind her, hurried out through the maze to see who was shouting for her this time.

It was Therandil.

"What are you doing here?" Cimorene said crossly. "I told you I wasn't going to be ready to be rescued for at least a month!"

"I was worried," Therandil said. "I heard that you'd broken a leg, but you look fine to me."

"Of course I haven't broken a leg," Cimorene said. "Where did you get that idea?"

"Some knight at the inn at the foot of the

mountain," Therandil replied. "He was up yesterday, talking to the princess he's trying to rescue, and he came back and warned everybody not to bother with the princess that was captured by the dragon Kazul. Well, I knew that was you, so I asked why, and he said his princess told him you'd broken your leg and wouldn't be able to walk for months."

Cimorene smiled slightly. Alianora had apparently gone through with her plan to tell Hallanna about Cimorene's "twisted ankle," and Hallanna had decided to improve the story a little in hopes of reducing the competition. "Somebody must have got mixed up," Cimorene said gently. "You can stop worrying. I'm fine. Is that all you came for? These jars are getting heavy, and I've got work to do."

"Cimorene, we have to talk," Therandil said in a heavy, deep voice.

"Then we'll have to do it while I work," Cimorene declared. She turned on her heel and marched into the kitchen, full of annoyance. She had been feeling almost friendly toward Therandil – he *had* been worried about her, after all – until he said he wanted to talk. Cimorene was quite sure that what he wanted to talk about was rescuing her, and she was annoyed with him for being so stupidly stubborn and annoyed with herself for being annoyed when he was only trying to do the best he could.

Therandil followed her into the kitchen. "What *is* all that?" he asked as Cimorene put the apron full of jars on the kitchen table and began lining them up.

"Some things I'm checking for Kazul," Cimorene said. She picked up a small jar made of carved jade and pried the lid off. It was half full of green salve. Cimorene put the lid back on and set the jar aside. "What was it you wanted to talk about?" she asked, reaching for another jar.

"You. Dragons. Us. That looks interesting. Can I help?"

"As long as you don't break anything," Cimorene said. "Some of these are very fragile." Maybe opening jars would make him forget about *You. Dragons. Us*, for a while.

"I'll be very careful," Therandil assured her. "This one looks like metal. I'll start with that, shall I?" He picked up one of the larger jars, made of beaten copper with two handles. He frowned at the top, then reached for his dagger, and as he tilted the jar, Cimorene saw that the neck was stopped up with lead.

"Not that one!" she said quickly. She didn't remember picking out that particular jar. It must have been one of the last four or five that she'd scooped up when she heard Therandil calling.

"Why not?" Therandil said, sounding rather hurt. "I said I'd be careful." The tip of his dagger was already embedded in the lead.

"Kazul said to leave the ones with lead stoppers alone," Cimorene said. "So put it back."

"If you insist," Therandil said, shrugging. He pulled on his dagger, but it was stuck fast in the lead. "Drat!" he said, and twisted the handle. The dagger came free, and the lead stopper came along with it.

"I should have known," Cimorene said in a resigned tone.

A black cloud of smoke poured out of the jar. As Cimorene and Therandil watched, it condensed into a dark-skinned giant wearing only a turban and a loincloth. He was more than twice as tall as Therandil, and the corners of his mouth were turned down in a stern frown.

"What is it?" whispered Therandil.

"Trouble," said Cimorene.

"Thou speakest truly, O Daughter of Wisdom," said the giant in a booming voice that filled the cave. "For I am a jinn, who was imprisoned in that jar, and I am the instrument of thy death and that of thy paramour."

"My *what?*" Cimorene said, outraged.

"Thy lover," the jinn said uncomfortably. "The man who stands beside thee."

"I know what you *meant*," Cimorene said. "But he isn't my lover, or my fiancé, or my boyfriend or anything, and I refuse to be killed with him."

"But Cimorene, you know perfectly well—" Therandil started.

"You hush," Cimorene said. "You've made enough of a mess already."

"If he is not thy paramour, nor any of those other things, then what is he?" the jinn asked suspiciously.

"A nuisance," Cimorene said succinctly.

"Cimorene, you're not being very kind," Therandil said.

"What he is matters not," the jinn said grandly after a moment's heavy thought. "It is enough that thou and he shall die."

"Enough for whom?" Cimorene said.

The jinn blinked at her. "For me. 'Tis my will that thou and he shall die by my hand. Thou hast but to choose the manner of thy death."

"Old age," Cimorene said promptly.

"Mock me not! Thou and he shall die, and by my hand, ere this day draws to its close!" the jinn cried.

"Do you suppose he means it?" Therandil said nervously.

"Why would he keep bellowing it at us if he didn't mean it?" Cimorene said. "Do be quiet, Therandil."

Therandil lowered his voice. "Should I offer to fight him, do you think?"

"Don't be silly," Cimorene said. She saw that Therandil was distressed, so she added, "You came up here to fight a dragon. You aren't prepared for a jinn, and nobody could reasonably expect you to challenge him."

"If you say so," Therandil said, looking relieved.

Cimorene turned back to the jinn and saw that he, too, was looking perturbed. "What's the matter with you?" she said crossly.

"Dost thou not wish to know *why* I will kill thee?" the jinn asked plaintively.

"What difference does it make?" Cimorene said.

"Yes, actually," Therandil said at the same time.

"Therandil!" Cimorene said in exasperation. "Shut *up!*"

"Hear my story, O luckless pair!" the jinn said with evident relief. "I am one of those jinn who did rebel against the law of our kind, and for my crimes I was sentenced to imprisonment in this bottle until the day should come when human hands would loose me. As is the custom of my people, I swore that whoso should release me during the first hundred years of my imprisonment I would make ruler of the earth; whoso should release me during the second hundred years I should make rich beyond all dreams of men; whoso shall release me during the third hundred I should grant three wishes; and whoso should release me after any longer span of time I should grant only the choice of what death he would die."

"You're going to kill us because it's *traditional?*" Cimorene asked.

"Yes," the jinn said. His eyes slid away from Cimorene's, and she frowned suddenly.

"Just how long were you in that jar?" she demanded.

"Uh, well, actually . . ." The jinn's voice trailed off.

"How long?" Cimorene insisted.

"Two hundred and seventeen years," the jinn admitted. "But nobody *ever* releases a jinn before the three hundred years are over."

"You're trying to get around your oath!" Therandil said, plainly shocked by the very thought. "You pretended you had to kill us so you wouldn't have to give us the wishes!"

"No!" the jinn said. "Thinkest thou that the granting of wishes alone would so trouble me? Needs must I kill thee and thy fair companion, for I cannot return home and say that thou didst release me and I left thee living! I would be a laughingstock. Never in three thousand years has such a thing occurred!"

"Then you shouldn't have sworn an oath," Therandil said sternly.

"I had to!" the jinn said miserably. "It is the custom of our kind. 'Twould be . . . 'twould be . . ."

"Improper?" Cimorene murmured.

"'Twould be improper to do otherwise," the jinn said, nodding. "But now thou hast found me out, and what am I to do? If I kill thee, it will violate my oath; if I kill thee not, the remainder of my life will be a torment."

"You could go back in the jar for another eighty-three years," Cimorene suggested delicately.

"I could . . . go back?" The jinn blinked at her for a moment. "I could go back. I could go back!"

"And in eighty-three years we'll both be dead of old age," Cimorene said. "Since that was my choice of death, your oath will be fulfilled and you can go straight home without killing anyone else or giving them any riches or power or anything."

"Truly, thou art a jewel among women and the very Queen of Wisdom's daughters!" the jinn said happily. "Thou hast found the perfect solution to my difficulties!"

"Wait a minute!" Therandil said. "What about those wishes?"

"Therandil!" Cimorene said in a shocked tone. "I'm surprised at you! How can he give us wishes if he's going back in the jar for eighty-three years? It wouldn't be right at all."

Therandil frowned. "Are you sure? After all, we *did* let him out during his third hundred years."

"I suppose I could let thee have one wish at least, in token of my thanks for thy help," the jinn said. "As long as thou dost not tell anyone."

"I wouldn't dream of it," Therandil assured him. "And my wish is to defeat a dragon and win his princess's hand in marriage!"

The jinn waved a dark hand over Therandil's head. "There! When next thou dost fight a dragon, thou shalt surely defeat him. And thou?" he said, turning to Cimorene.

"I could use some powdered hens' teeth," Cimorene said.

The jinn blinked in surprise, but he waved his hand again, his face a mask of concentration. Then he bowed and handed Cimorene a fat brown jar. "There's thy desire. Farewell!" With an elaborate salaam, the jinn dissolved back into a cloud of smoke that poured back into the copper jar from which it had come. Cimorene leaned over and plucked the lead stopper from the end of Therandil's knife. She jammed it back into place and heaved a sigh of relief.

Therandil was not paying attention. "What did you want something like that for?" he asked, looking at the jar of hens' teeth and wrinkling his nose in distaste.

"I don't believe I shall tell you," Cimorene said, putting the jar carefully into one of her apron pockets. "It has nothing to do with you."

"Nothing to do with me? I like that!" Therandil said indignantly. "I'm going to marry you, just as soon as I beat that dragon of yours."

"I don't think you're going to beat Kazul," Cimorene said in a considering tone.

"But that jinn just said—"

"He said that if you fight a dragon, you'll defeat him. But Kazul is a her, not a him," Cimorene pointed out. "And you ought not to be trying to rescue me anyway."

"Why not?" Therandil asked truculently.

"Because there are other princesses who've been captives of dragons for much longer than I have, and they have seniority," Cimorene explained.

"Oh," said Therandil, looking considerably taken aback. "How do you know?"

"They came to visit and told me all about

it," Cimorene said. "I think you should try for Keredwel. She's from the Kingdom of Raxwel, and her hair is the color of sun-ripened wheat, and she wears a gold crown set with diamonds. You ought to get along with her very well."

Therandil brightened perceptibly at this description but said, "But everyone expects me to rescue *you.*"

"As long as you defeat a dragon and rescue a princess, no one will care," Cimorene said firmly. "And Keredwel will suit you much better than I would."

"Are you sure her dragon isn't female, too?"

"Positive," Cimorene said. "Gornul's cave is two down and three over. If you follow the path outside, you can't miss it. He ought to be there now, and if you leave right away, you'll be able to get everything settled before dinner."

"All right, then," Therandil said. "As long as you're sure you don't mind."

"Not at all," Cimorene assured him fervently. She saw him to the mouth of the cave and pointed him toward Gornul's cave, then returned to the kitchen. She gathered up the jars and bottles she had been planning to check, except for the copper jar with the jinn inside, and took them back to the treasure vault. Then she fetched an ink pot, a quill pen, and a sheet of paper from the library and began writing out a warning to attach to the copper jar. She didn't want anyone else to open it until the eighty-three years were over and the jinn could go home without killing anyone.

She was just finishing when she heard Alianora's voice calling from the rear of the cave. "I'm in the kitchen!" she shouted. "Come on back!"

"You're always in the kitchen," Alianora said when she poked her head through the door a moment later. "Or the library. Don't you ever do anything but cook and read?"

"Look at this, Alianora," Cimorene said, handing her the warning she had been writing. "Do you think it's clear enough?"

" 'WARNING: This jar contains a jinn who will kill you if you let him out too soon. Do not open until at least one hundred and five years after the date when the Citadel of the Yellow Giant was destroyed,' " Alianora read aloud. "That's, let's see, eighty-four years from now. It seems clear to me. You'd have to be pretty stupid to ignore a warning like that."

"Maybe I ought to show it to Hallanna and see what she says," Cimorene said, frowning. "I wouldn't want anyone getting into trouble by accident, just because I didn't make it plain."

"It's plain, it's plain," Alianora said. "Cimorene, what on *earth* have you been doing? How do you know there's a jinn in this bottle?"

"Therandil," Cimorene said, waving a hand expressively. "I was looking through some of the bottles from Kazul's treasure room, to see if any of them happened to have hens' teeth in them, and Therandil came in and wanted to help."

"And he opened it?" Alianora said. "Oh, dear."

"Exactly," said Cimorene. "But it came out well in the end. I think I've got rid of him for good. I sent him off to rescue Keredwel."

"You *did*? What if he doesn't beat Gornul?"

"Oh, he'll win. The jinn gave him a wish, and he wished to defeat a dragon." Cimorene looked apologetically at Alianora. "I suppose I ought to have sent him to rescue you, but . . ."

"That's quite all right," Alianora said hastily. "Getting rid of Keredwel will help a lot. And after everything you've told me about Therandil, I don't think I'd want to have him rescue me."

"That's what I thought," Cimorene said. "Oh, and I got the jinn to give me some powdered hens' teeth, so we can finally try that fireproofing spell."

"Good," Alianora said. "Let's do it right now!"

So Cimorene got out the spell and the ingredients she had collected, and she and Alianora spent the next hour on various necessary preparations. First they had to boil some unicorn water and steep the dried wolfsbane in it. Then the mixture had to be strained and mixed with the hippopotamus oil and the powdered hens' teeth. Cimorene did most of that, while Alianora ground up the blue rose leaves and the piece of ebony.

Grinding the ebony took a long time, but fortunately they didn't need much. When Alianora finally had enough, Cimorene mixed it with the blue rose leaves and more of the unicorn water in one of Kazul's recently shed scales. Each mixture had to be stirred three times counterclockwise with a white eagle feather. Then Alianora dipped the point of her feather in her mixture and began drawing a star on the floor of the cave.

"Is this going to be big enough for both of us?" she asked, scratching busily at the stone with the tip of the feather.

"I think so," Cimorene answered. "Don't try to make it too big, or you'll run out of liquid and we'll have to start over."

Alianora did not run out, though she had used nearly all her mixture by the time she finished. "There!" she said. She sat back on her heels and studied her diagram to make sure there were no gaps, then set her dragon scale and feather aside and stood up. "Your turn."

"First we have to get into the center of the star," Cimorene reminded her. "Be careful not to smudge the lines!"

"Smudge them, after all that work?" Alianora said in tones of mock horror. She lifted her skirts and stepped carefully into the middle of the diagram. Cimorene followed, carrying a small mixing bowl half full of something that looked like brown sludge with a white eagle feather sticking out of one side. "It smells awful," Alianora said, grimacing.

"It doesn't matter what it smells like, as long as the spell works," Cimorene said. "Ready?"

"As ready as I'm ever going to be," Alianora replied, shutting her eyes and screwing up her face as if she expected to have a glass of cold water poured over her head.

Cimorene plucked the eagle feather out of the bowl and raised it quickly over Alianora's head before it could drip on the floor. She let four large drops of the brown gunk fall onto Alianora's hair, then brushed the end of the feather across her forehead twice. She finished by drawing a circle with the feather on the palm of Alianora's left hand.

"That tickles!" Alianora complained.

"Well, you can do it to me now," Cimorene said.

Alianora took the bowl and feather from Cimorene.

"You're right," Cimorene said a moment later. "It does tickle."

"Now what?" Alianora said.

"Set the bowl down and shut your eyes," Cimorene instructed. When Alianora had done so, Cimorene closed her own eyes and said:

> *"Power of water, wind and earth,*
> *Turn the fire back to its birth.*
> *Raise the spell to shield the flame*
> *By the power that we have tamed."*

"Oh!" said Alianora. "That feels *peculiar*. Can I open my eyes now?"

"Yes," said Cimorene, opening her own. "We're finished."

"Did it work?" Alianora asked, cautiously opening one eye and squinting at Cimorene.

"Well, *something* happened. We both felt it," Cimorene said. "And your hair and forehead don't have brown gunk on them any more."

Alianora promptly opened both eyes and studied Cimorene. "Neither do yours. What does that mean?"

"It means we go back to the kitchen and test it," Cimorene said. She bent over and picked up the mixing bowl. "We'll clean up later. Come on."

CHAPTER 1º

*In Which Cimorene and Alianora Conduct
Some Tests and Disturb a Wizard*

Back in the kitchen, Cimorene and Alianora quickly determined that the fireproofing spell had indeed worked. First Cimorene, then Alianora tossed a pinch of feverfew into the air and recited the spell-verse, then put a hand into a candle flame and held it there. Neither was burned at all, though Alianora claimed that the candle tickled almost as much as the eagle feather had done.

"How long does the spell last?" Alianora asked.

"I'm not sure, exactly," Cimorene said. "At least an hour, but I'll have to do some tests to pin it down beyond that. I hope Kazul gets back soon. I want to see if it works with dragon fire."

"You're going to have Kazul breathe fire at you, just to see if the spell works?" Alianora said, horrified. "What if it doesn't?"

"Then I'll talk to Kazul, and we'll go see Morwen, and the three of us will try to figure out what to change to make the spell work for dragon fire, too. Don't look at me like that. I'm not going to stand in front of Kazul and have her breathe fire at me. I'll just stick out a finger, the way we did with the candle."

This was not enough to convince Alianora, but Cimorene was determined. "The whole point of trying this spell was to make ourselves immune to dragon fire," she said. "If it doesn't work, I don't want to find out for the first time when one of Kazul's guests gets mad and breathes fire at me because he doesn't like the way I cooked his cherries jubilee."

Alianora had to admit that this was a good point, but she was still disposed to argue. The discussion was cut short by Kazul's return. At first the dragon was more inclined to agree with Alianora than with Cimorene, but after Cimorene proved her invulnerability to candle flames, lighted torches, and the fire she had built in the kitchen stove, Kazul agreed to the trial. She insisted, however, on working up to full firepower in gradual stages, and Cimorene was forced to agree.

Before they began, Cimorene threw another pinch of feverfew into the air and recited the couplet again, just to be sure the spell wouldn't wear off in the middle of the test. Then Kazul lowered her head nearly to the ground, and Alianora watched nervously as Cimorene lowered her hand slowly into various intensities of dragon flame. Finally, Cimorene stood right in front of Kazul while the dragon breathed her hottest. The spell worked perfectly every time.

"There!" Cimorene said when Kazul stopped at last. "Now we know it works. Aren't you glad?"

"I'm glad," Alianora said fervently. "And I hope I never have to watch anything like that again as long as I live. I didn't dare blink for fear you'd go up in smoke while my eyes were closed."

"Why don't you try it yourself?" Cimorene said mischievously.

"No!" said Alianora and Kazul together.

"Watching you was bad enough," Alianora went on with a shudder. "I believe it works. I don't see any reason for me to test it."

"Besides, I've done more than enough fire-breathing for one day," Kazul added. "I'm starting to get overheated."

"All right, if you don't want to, you don't have to," Cimorene said. "If we're all done, I'd better go tidy up."

Alianora stayed to help Cimorene finish cleaning up the traces of the spell, by which time she had calmed down considerably and was very nearly her usual self again. Cimorene gave her a pouchful of dried feverfew before she left and made her recite the words that activated the spell several times, to make sure she had memorized them correctly.

"Remember, you only have to repeat the first half of the verse to get the spell going, now that it's been set up," Cimorene said. "Can you do it?"

"It's only two lines, and they rhyme!" Alianora said, laughing. "How could I forget that? My memory isn't that bad!"

"Maybe not, but say it anyway," Cimorene said. Alianora laughed again and did so. At last she set off into the tunnels, and Cimorene went back to the main cave to see what Kazul and Roxim had found out about the Caves of Fire and Night.

Kazul was somewhat out of temper, and Cimorene thought privately that she had been telling the truth about getting overheated. Rather than annoy the dragon further, Cimorene asked if she could read the book Kazul had borrowed from Morwen.

"It's in the treasure room," Kazul said. "Read it there. And I hope you see something in it that we didn't."

Cimorene nodded, picked up her lamp, and hurried off before Kazul could change her mind. The book was lying near a pile of sapphires, next to an ornate gold crown. She picked it up, went over to the table, which was large and very sturdy because it was intended for counting piles of gold and silver coins, and sat down to read.

It was even dryer and duller than Kazul had said. There were a great many "mayhaps" and "perchances" and "wherefores," strung together in long, involved sentences that compared the strange and wonderful things in the caves to obscure philosophical ideas and odd customs from places Cimorene had never heard of. After a few pages, Cimorene put the book down and went and got a quill pen, an ink pot, and some paper, so that she could write down the things she thought were important. She didn't want to have to read *A Journey Through the Caves of Fire and Night* more than once.

For the next three days, Cimorene spent bits of her spare time in the treasure room, taking notes on the DeMontmorency. It took her that long because she could never manage to read for more than a little while without getting so bored that she nearly fell asleep. Her persisttence gained her several pages of notes about the caves, but nothing that seemed as if it might be of particular interest to wizards.

Alianora came to see her a few days later, looking very cheerful.

"It worked!" she announced as she came into the library where Cimorene was going over her notes. "Keredwel's gone. Therandil rescued her, just the way you said he would."

"Good," Cimorene said. "I'm glad something is going right."

"What's the problem?" Alianora asked, seating herself on the other side of the table from Cimorene.

"This," Cimorene said, waving at the paper-covered table. "Kazul is sure that the key to what the wizards are after is somewhere in that dratted book she borrowed from Morwen. I copied out everything that looked interesting, but none of it seems like anything a wizard would care about."

"How do you know that?" Alianora asked curiously.

"I don't," Cimorene said. "I'm just guessing. That's the problem."

"Oh." Alianora picked up the sheet of paper

nearest her and frowned at it. "What on earth does this mean?"

Cimorene looked at the page Alianora was holding. "'Thus these Caves of Fire and Night are, in some sense, indivisible, whereas the Caves of Chance are, by contrast, individual, though it is preposterous to claim that these descriptions are true of either group of caves in their entirety . . .' That's one of the bits I copied word for word; the whole book is like that. I think it means that if you have a piece of something magical from the Caves of Fire and Night, you can use it in a spell as if it were the whole thing."

"I can see why you wouldn't be sure," Alianora said. "Do you think it would help you figure things out if you stopped for a while?"

"I have stopped," Cimorene pointed out. "Or did you have something more specific in mind?"

"I'm almost out of feverfew," Alianora said, looking down at the table. "I was hoping you'd come with me to pick some more."

"You're almost *out?*" Cimorene said in surprise. "How did that happen?"

Alianora shifted uncomfortably. "I've been working that fireproofing spell every hour or so for the past two days," she admitted. "Woraug has been getting more and more unpredictable, and I don't feel comfortable otherwise. Hallanna was visiting yesterday when he came in – in the middle of the afternoon! – and he was roaring and dripping little bits of flame when he breathed. She was terrified, and I don't blame her. If it weren't for the spell, I'd be scared to death."

"What's the matter with him?"

"I don't know. He doesn't tell me anything about dragon politics or wizards or what he's been getting so worked up about. He's not like Kazul."

Cimorene frowned, considering. "Maybe Kazul will have some idea what's bothering him. I'll ask her this evening. In the meantime, let's go get that feverfew. You're right to say that I could use a break."

"Oh, good," said Alianora in tones of considerable relief. "I've never picked herbs before, and I'm not sure what feverfew looks like. I don't know what I'd have done if you'd said you wouldn't come."

Cimorene put her notes away and got two wicker baskets and a small knife from one of the storage rooms. "Up or down?" Alianora asked as they left the cave.

"Up," Cimorene said. "The other way is the ledge I told you about, and I wouldn't be surprised if bits of it are still invisible."

*   *   *

The path through the Pass of Silver Ice twisted and turned past the openings of other dragons' caves. Most of the rocks around the caves had scorch marks, and Cimorene and Alianora didn't see much growing among them.

"At this rate, we'll have to go nearly all the way to the Enchanted Forest to find any grass, much less herbs!" Alianora complained.

"Wait a minute!" Cimorene said. "Look over there, through that crack in the rocks. Doesn't that look like something green?"

Alianora's eyes followed Cimorene's pointing finger. "Yes," she said without enthusiasm. "It looks green."

The rock Cimorene had indicated was a large boulder at the bottom of a steep slope. The slope was covered with gravel and looked as if it would be impossible to climb down without skinning a knee or an elbow at the very least. The boulder itself was in two pieces, with just enough space between them for someone to squeeze through, provided the someone was not very large.

"Come on, let's get a better look," said Cimorene. She walked to the edge of the slope and wrapped her skirts tightly around her legs. Then she sat down with her basket in her lap and slid down the slope, raising an enormous cloud of dust and sounding like an avalanche in process. She reached the bottom in safety and stood up, brushing at her skirt. The dust was so thick that she could hardly see, and when she tried to call to Alianora, she coughed so hard that she could barely speak.

"Cimorene! Are you all right?"

"It's just the dust," Cimorene said in a muffled voice. She had taken out her handkerchief and put it over her mouth and nose to keep the dust out. It wasn't perfect, but it helped a great deal. "Come on, it's your turn."

"Are you sure we shouldn't just go around?"

"Stop stalling. It's not that bad."

"That's what you say," Alianora muttered, but she wrapped her skirts around her, clutched her basket, and slid down the slope. She made even more noise than Cimorene had. When she got to the bottom, she was coughing and choking. Cimorene handed her the handkerchief, and they waited for a moment while the dust settled.

Crawling through the split boulder was easier than they expected. The crevice was wider than it had looked from the path, and the bottom of the crack was so full of dust and gravel and dead leaves that it was almost flat. Cimorene and Alianora had to walk single file, and there were one or two spots where they had to turn sideways in order to get through, but it was not really difficult.

On the other side of the boulder, the two girls found a lush, green valley. It was bowl-shaped and not very large, but flowers and grasses stood waist-high between the random clumps of bushes that dotted the valley floor. A squirrel, which had been sunning itself on a ledge near the entrance, leaped for a small tree as Cimorene and Alianora appeared.

"My goodness!" Alianora said, looking around with wide eyes. "This place looks as if no one but us has ever been here before. There aren't even any scorch marks on the rocks."

Cimorene blinked. Alianora was right. Lichens covered the weathered gray rocks that rose above the valley, and small plants grew in cracks and crevices that showed no sign of the touch of dragon fire.

"That's odd," Cimorene commented.

"Why?" Alianora asked.

"Those mountains aren't tall enough to keep dragons from flying over, and they're right in the middle of the dragons' territory. So why haven't the dragons been here? They usually keep a close eye on everything that belongs to them."

"Maybe they have been here, but they never found anything to breathe fire at," Alianora said.

"Well, I'm going to ask Kazul about it when I get back," Cimorene said as she waded into the grass. "Why don't you take that side, and I'll look over here? We'll cover more ground that way."

"First you'd better show me what I'm looking for," Alianora said apologetically. "I'm afraid I couldn't tell feverfew from carrots if there was a dragon chasing me and my life depended on it."

Cimorene nodded, and they started off. They had not gone far when she saw a patch of the white button-shaped flowers she was looking for. "Here," she said, showing them to Alianora. "This is feverfew. The younger plants are the best, the ones that haven't blossomed yet."

Alianora studied the leaves and flowers with care. "I think I'll recognize it now."

They cut some of the plants, leaving those that were blooming.

"You find the next patch," Cimorene said as they started off again.

"Let's try over there," Alianora said, pointing.

They found several more patches of feverfew, and gradually their baskets began to fill. "I think this should be enough," Cimorene said at least. "Unless you think—"

"Cimorene!" Alianora hissed, clutching at Cimorene's arm. "There someone behind that bush!"

Cimorene turned. A dark line snaked through the grass where something large had bent and broken the plants in passing. "You're right," she said, and started forward.

Alianora hung back, still holding Cimorene's arm. "You're not going to go *look*, are you?"

"How else are we going to find out who it is?" Cimorene asked reasonably. She shook off Alianora's hand. Quietly, she walked over to the clump of bushes and peered around it. Alianora followed with evident reluctance.

A man in blue and brown silk robes was crouched on the other side of the bush with his back toward Cimorene. He was stuffing saw-edged purple leaves into a small linen bag the size of Cimorene's hand. His hair was brown, and on the ground beside him lay a long, polished staff.

"Antorell?" Cimorene said in surprise.

The man snatched up his staff and straightened as if a bee had just stung him. It was indeed Antorell, and he did not look at all pleased to see her. He stuffed the linen bag quickly into his sleeve and said, "P-princess Cimorene! What brings you here?"

"I was about to ask you the same thing," Cimorene said.

"Wizards go where they wish, answering to

no one," Antorell said, waving his free hand in a lofty manner.

"Maybe outside the Mountains of Morning they do, but around here they have to check with the dragons first," Cimorene said.

"You know nothing of the matter," Antorell said, looking very put out.

"Cimorene . . ." Alianora's tone was doubtful. "You know this person?"

"I'm sorry; I should have introduced you. This is Antorell, one of the wizards I told you about. Antorell, this is Princess Alianora of the Duchy of Toure-on-Marsh. At the moment, she's the princess of the dragon Woraug."

Alianora curtsied, murmuring something polite and inaudible. Antorell, who had stiffened in surprise when he realized that Cimorene was not alone, relaxed visibly. "Woraug's princess? That's all right, then. Though he really shouldn't have sent you."

"But Woraug didn't – ow!" said Alianora. The "ow" was because Cimorene had hastily kicked her ankle to keep her from telling Antorell too much.

"Didn't what?" Antorell asked, frowning suspiciously.

"Didn't know you were going to be here," Cimorene said.

"Well, of course he didn't know!" Antorell

said, looking annoyed. "That's the whole point, after all."

Cimorene would have very much liked to ask him what the point was, but she was afraid it would make him suspicious again. "I don't understand," she said instead, batting her eyes at him.

"Of course not," Antorell replied in a condescending tone that made Cimorene's teeth hurt. "But it doesn't matter. I'm not annoyed with you."

"I'm so glad," Cimorene murmured.

Antorell gave her an oily smile. "In fact, there's no need for you to tell Woraug that you met me here."

"I wouldn't dream of it," Cimorene said with perfect truth.

"Excellent," Antorell said. "Then may I escort the two of you back to the path?"

Alianora looked hopefully in Cimorene's direction.

"But we can't leave yet," Cimorene said, opening her eyes very wide. "We haven't picked any cornflowers or daisies." Behind her, she heard Alianora making a smothered, choking noise, as if she were trying very hard not to laugh.

"Daisies," Antorell said in a flat, incredulous tone. "You want to stay and pick daisies?"

Cimorene nodded vigorously. "And corn-flowers, and flax, and all sorts of things," she said, waving her hand at the flowers blooming all around. "They'll look so pretty in a bowl of water in the kitchen."

"I'm sure you're right," Antorell said. He looked as if he would have liked to object, but couldn't think of anything to object to. "Perhaps I could help you?" he said reluctantly.

"Oh, we wouldn't dream of keeping you," Cimorene said.

Antorell was clearly reluctant to leave the two girls in the valley, but Cimorene did not give him much choice. After another minute or so of conversation, the wizard was forced to go. He did not use a vanishing spell but trudged away on foot. Cimorene watched him until he was out of sight among the bushes, wondering whether he had some special reason not to use spells in the valley or whether he simply didn't know the right spells to make himself vanish.

"That's a relief!" Alianora said. "Why did you insist on staying when it was so obvious that he wanted us to leave? I was afraid he was going to turn us into toads or something."

"I wanted to see what he was up to," Cimorene said. "And I don't think Antorell is a very good wizard. He probably couldn't manage anything worse than a squirrel."

Alianora did not appear to find this very reassuring. Cimorene checked to make sure Antorell was out of sight, then went over to the place where he had been standing when she peered around the bush. At first she did not notice anything unusual. Then she saw a purplish plant oozing sap from the places where several of its spiky, saw-toothed leaves had been broken off.

"Look at this."

"What is it?" Alianora asked.

"I don't know," Cimorene said absently. "I saw a couple of other plants like this while we were picking feverfew, but I thought they were just weeds."

"Maybe it is a weed."

"A wizard wouldn't sneak into the dragon's section of the Mountains of Morning just to pick weeds. They don't even use herbs to cast spells, so what does Antorell want with this prickly looking thing?"

Alianora shrugged. "Maybe he needs it for something he can't do with magic."

"I wonder what that would be?" Cimorene reached out and carefully broke off a spray of leaves. She wrapped them in her handkerchief and put the packet in her pocket. "Let's see if we can find out whether he picked anything else."

Antorell had left a dark trail of bent and broken plants to mark the way he had come, so his path was easy to follow. Cimorene and Alianora searched carefully along it for some way, looking for signs that the wizard had picked other herbs, but neither of them saw any.

"I don't think there's anything to find," Alianora said, pushing her apricot-colored hair out of her face. "And it's getting awfully warm."

"Have you noticed that there aren't any of those purple plants along here?" Cimorene said. "I'll bet that was all he wanted."

"Then let's leave before that wizard thinks to circle around to check on what we're doing," Alianora urged.

Cimorene doubted that Antorell would think of doing such a thing, but she nodded agreement, and the two girls left the valley. Alianora was quiet and thoughtful for most of the walk back to Kazul's cave. Cimorene was grateful for the silence. She had a lot to think about herself. From what Antorell had said, it seemed likely that Woraug was helping the wizards somehow, or at least that he had known what Antorell was looking for in the little valley. Cimorene found it difficult to imagine a dragon helping a wizard, but she couldn't say with certainty that it was impossible. And if Woraug *was* involved with

Antorell and Zemenar, it might explain why he had been so touchy lately.

When they arrived back at the cave, Cimorene shook herself free of her preoccupation. She and Alianora unloaded their baskets and tied the herbs in bunches to hang in a dark corner of the kitchen to dry.

"How long will it be before I can use the feverfew?" Alianora asked worriedly.

"I'm not sure," Cimorene said in a considering tone. "It will take at least a week to dry thoroughly, but you might be able to use it in the spell before then. The directions don't say how dry the feverfew has to be. We could try it every day with a pinch of leaves from one of the bunches if you like."

Alianora nodded. "I really do need it."

"I wonder if it would work without being dried?" Cimorene said. She pulled a leaf from one of the hanging plants and shredded it carefully between her fingers, then tossed it up in the air and recited the rhyme. "There! Now, light a candle or another lamp or something."

Alianora had already lit a candle and set it on the table. Cimorene moved over and stuck her finger in the flame.

"I think it's working," she said, and moved the rest of her hand closer.

The sleeve of her dress caught fire. Cimorene hastily pulled her hand away from the candle and slapped at the flames, while Alianora snatched up a bucket of water from beside the sink and poured it over Cimorene's arm. The fire went out and so did the candle, and both Cimorene and Alianora got thoroughly soaked.

"Oh, dear!" Alianora said, ignoring her soggy skirts. "Cimorene, did you burn yourself?"

"No," Cimorene said, looking at her arm with a puzzled expression. "I didn't feel a thing. I thought the spell worked, but nothing caught fire when we tested it before."

"It must be because the feverfew is fresh instead of dried. And I *hoped* that I'd be able to use it right away!"

"If you're that low on dried feverfew, take some of mine," Cimorene offered. "Kazul's not particularly irritable. I only need to keep a pinch or two in case of emergencies."

"Thank you!" Alianora said fervently, and Cimorene turned her soggy cuffs back and went to get the bottled spices.

Chapter 11

In Which Kazul Is Unwell, and Cimorene Makes a New Acquaintance

Alianora decided to return home by way of the path outside instead of through the tunnels because it was such a nice day and she hoped the sun would dry her skirt. Cimorene watched her go, swinging her basket happily and humming a little, her confidence and good humor completely restored by the possession of the fat little packet of dried feverfew in her pocket.

"I wish I had as little to worry about," Cimorene muttered, thinking of Woraug and the wizards. She held the burned patch at the end of her sleeve up to get a better look at it in the sunlight and shook her head. Even the magic

170

wardrobe would have a hard time fixing that. A puff of wind made her shiver in her wet clothes, and she turned to go back into the cave to change.

A dark shadow fell over Cimorene, and she stopped and looked up. "Kazul!" she said as the dragon landed on the open path beside her. "Am I glad to see you. Wait until you hear what's been happening!"

"You do appear to have had a rather strenuous day," Kazul said, eyeing Cimorene's wet, stained skirt and the blackened end of her right sleeve. "Nothing serious, I trust?"

"I'm not sure," Cimorene said. "Alianora and I went out to pick some feverfew, and we ran into that wizard Antorell."

"Where was this?"

Cimorene pointed. "Up that way. There's a little round valley off to one side that looks as if dragons never go there, and—"

"You found a wizard *there?*" Kazul sounded deeply disturbed. "How did he get in? How did *you* get in?"

"We climbed through a crack in a boulder," Cimorene said. "I don't know how Antorell did it. When he left, he was heading for the far side of the valley."

"This is serious," Kazul said, getting to her

feet. "I'd better warn the King. He'll have to use the crystal now."

"You'd better hear the rest of it first," Cimorene said. "Antorell wasn't too happy to see us, but when he found out that Alianora was Woraug's princess, he relaxed. He seemed to think that Woraug had sent us."

"What?"

Cimorene involuntarily stepped back a pace at the anger in Kazul's voice. "He thought Woraug had sent us," she repeated, and gave a quick summary of her conversation with Antorell.

"Woraug!" Kazul's tail lashed, sweeping a small boulder from one side of the path to the other. "But Woraug's not a fool, and only a fool would let a wizard into that valley. Unless he was sure that they didn't know . . . What was Antorell doing?"

"Cutting plants," Cimorene said. "Or rather, cutting *a* plant. It didn't look as if he took more than one."

"He wouldn't need more than one, if it was the right one," Kazul said tensely. "What did he pick?"

"It was a prickly looking purple thing, with saw-edged leaves," Cimorene said, reaching into her pocket. "I didn't recognize it, but I thought you might, so I brought a piece back for you to look—"

"What?" Kazul roared.

Flame spurted from the dragon's mouth, enveloping Cimorene. Steam hissed from her wet skirt, and the thinner material of her sleeves vanished in a crackle of sparks. The handkerchief-wrapped spray of purple leaves, which she had just taken out of her pocket to show Kazul, disintegrated into a dark, greasy-looking cloud of smoke.

Cimorene stared at the ashes in her palm, feeling very, very glad that she had decided to test the way fresh feverfew would work in the fireproofing spell. She felt a little warm, and her clothes had been reduced to a few charred rags, but that was nothing compared to what might have happened.

"Now I understand why Alianora ran out of feverfew," she muttered.

A puff of wind brushed Cimorene's arms, and she heard a choking sound from Kazul. She looked up, expecting to find the dragon laughing at her remark, and her eyes widened. Kazul's head was thrown back, and her mouth was wide open, giving Cimorene an excellent view of the dragon's sharp silver teeth and long red tongue. Cimorene skipped backward out of reach; then she realized that the dragon was gasping for air.

"Kazul! What's the matter?"

"The smoke!" Kazul coughed. Her voice was so hoarse that it was hard for Cimorene to understand what she was saying.

"What can I do?" Cimorene said, trying not to feel frightened.

"Green jar – shelf in last treasure room," Kazul managed between coughs. "Hurry."

Cimorene was already running through the mouth of the cave as fast as her feet could carry her. She did not even pause as she snatched up her lamp from the floor just inside the door. It seemed to take forever to get through the twisty passages and the first two caves full of treasure. She skidded to a halt in the doorway of the third room and stood panting, scanning the walls for the shelf and the right jar. She found it quickly and ran back at once, the jar clutched tightly in her right hand.

The sound of Kazul's coughing grew louder as Cimorene sped back the way she had come. At the mouth of the cave, Cimorene paused and set down the lamp, then unscrewed the top of the green jar. Inside was a thick, emerald-colored liquid about the consistency of honey. She looked out at Kazul. The dragon's head jerked with each cough, and the scales on her neck were beginning to turn pink around the edges. For a long, careful moment Cimorene studied Kazul's movements. Then she leaned back and threw the emerald liquid, jar and all, into the dragon's open mouth just as Kazul took another gasping breath.

The jar landed on Kazul's tongue. The dragon's mouth closed, and she swallowed convulsively. Sudden silence descended.

"Are you all right now?" Cimorene asked after Kazul had taken several deep breaths without a renewed bout of coughing.

"I will be," Kazul said. She sounded exhausted, and her movements as she slid into the cave were slow and uncertain.

"What happened?" Cimorene said, backing out of the way so that Kazul would not have to exert herself to go around.

"I got a breath of the smoke when the plant in your hand burned," Kazul said as she settled to the floor just inside the entrance. "Lucky it was only a breath. I'll need a few days of rest, but that's better than being dead."

Cimorene stared at her, appalled. "What *was* that plant?"

"Dragonsbane," said Kazul. Her eyes closed and she slept.

Kazul continued to sleep for most of the next three days. She woke only long enough for Cimorene to pour a couple of gallons of warm milk mixed with honey down her throat from time to time before she lapsed back into unconsciousness. Cimorene was very worried, but there wasn't much that she could do. Sick dragons are too large and heavy for normal nursing to be of much use.

On the afternoon of the third day, Kazul woke up completely for the first time since her collapse.

"Thank goodness!" said Cimorene as Kazul shook her head experimentally and sat up. "I was beginning to think you were going to sleep for a month."

"I might have if I'd gotten more than a whiff of that smoke." Kazul stretched her neck in one direction and her tail in the other, trying to work out some of the kinks.

"If I'd known it was so dangerous, I'd never have brought any of that purple plant back with me," Cimorene apologized. "You might have done worse than sleep for a month. You might have—" She stopped, unwilling to complete the thought.

"I might have died?" Kazul said. "Unlikely. If a dragon isn't killed outright by something in the first five minutes, recovery is only a matter of time. That applies as much to dragonsbane as to a knight's magic sword."

"Then why did you want that goo in the green jar?" Cimorene asked.

"The antidote? I wanted it because I didn't like the idea of spending a month recuperating when I didn't have to. And since—" A fit of coughing interrupted Kazul in mid-sentence.

Cimorene skipped backward out of the way. Frowning worriedly, she tossed a pinch of feverfew into the air and recited the verse from the fireproofing spell in case Kazul should lose control of her flame again. "Maybe you won't need a month to recover, but three days obviously isn't enough," she said to the dragon. "You'd better lie back down before you choke."

"I can't," Kazul said. "I have to warn the King. If the wizards have had dragonsbane for three days already—" She started coughing again and had to stop talking.

"You stay here," Cimorene said in a firm tone. "I'll warn the King."

"Tokoz won't listen to you," Kazul said, but she settled back to the ground. "Roxim will, though. Start with him."

"Roxim?" Cimorene said doubtfully. She was afraid the gray-green dragon would want to go charging out after the wizards as soon as he heard they were up to something.

"He'll listen to you, and the King will listen to him," Kazul said. "It's not ideal, but it's the best we can do."

"All right, I'll go see Roxim. You stay here and sleep."

"When you get back—"

"I'll wake you and tell you what he said," Cimorene promised. "Now, *go to sleep.*"

Kazul smiled slightly and closed her eyes. Cimorene caught up a lamp and almost ran to the exit at the back of the cave. She was afraid that Kazul would think of something else and start talking again, and she didn't think talking would be good for her.

In the tunnel outside, Cimorene paused, trying to remember the directions to Roxim's cave. She had memorized a map in the library that showed most of the twists and turns of the dragons' tunnels, but she knew from experience that in the miles of gray stone corridors it was difficult to keep track of where she was.

"Left, left, fifth right, past the little chamber, right again, on past the iron gate, two lefts to the third cave down," she muttered to herself. "I *wish* Roxim's cave were closer." Still muttering, she started off.

Though she was being very careful, Cimorene had to backtrack twice during the first part of her trip when a mistake in counting corridors led her to a dead end. When she finally saw the iron gate that led into the Caves of Fire and Night, she sighed in relief. The tricky part was over, and the rest of the trip would be easy. She held her lamp up and quickened her step, hoping to make up some of the time she had lost on her detours. Then, as she reached the bars that blocked the entrance to the Caves of Fire and Night, she stopped short. There was someone sitting on the ground on the other side of the gate.

Cimorene had almost missed seeing him, and no wonder. His clothes, though well cut, were the same dark gray as the stone of the tunnel walls, and he was curled into a lumpy, dejected ball. He looked like a large rock. If he hadn't moved his hand as she passed, Cimorene would never have realized he was alive.

The man on the other side of the bars raised his head, and Cimorene saw with shock that his hair and skin were the same dark, even gray as his clothes. His eyes, too, were gray and their expression was apologetic.

"Forgive me for startling you," the man said, climbing ponderously to his feet. "I didn't see you coming." He made a stiff, formal bow.

"Who are you?" Cimorene demanded. "And what are you doing in there?"

"I'm a prince," the man said in a gloomy tone, "and I'm reaping the rewards of my folly."

"What folly?"

The prince sighed. "It's a long story."

"Somehow they always seem to be long," Cimorene said. "You haven't come to rescue me from the dragons, have you? Because if you have, I'm not going to let you out of there. I haven't got time to spend an hour arguing today."

"I have no interest whatever in dragons, I assure you," the prince said earnestly. "And if you would let me out, I'd be extremely grateful. Um, who are you, by the way?"

"Cimorene, princess of the dragon Kazul," Cimorene said. She studied the prince for a moment and decided that he looked trustworthy. "All right, I'll let you out. Turn around and put your fingers in your ears."

"What?" the prince said, looking considerably startled.

"It's part of the spell to open the gate," Cimorene said. She wasn't about to let him overhear the words Kazul had used to unlock the door, even if he did look trustworthy.

The prince shrugged and did as she directed. Quickly, Cimorene recited:

"By night and flame and shining rock
Open thou thy hidden lock.
Alberolingarn!"

For an instant nothing happened, and Cimorene was afraid she had not remembered the charm correctly. Then the iron gate swung silently open. The prince, whose back was to the gate, did not notice. Cimorene touched his shoulder to get his attention, and her eyes widened.

"Oh!" she said as he turned. "You're – you're *stone*."

"I know," the prince said. "It's part of that long story I mentioned earlier. I'm not used to it yet." He stepped through the gate, and it closed noiselessly behind him.

"I'm afraid I don't have time to listen to stories just now," Cimorene said politely. "I have a rather urgent errand to run, so if you'll excuse me—"

"Can't I come with you?"

Cimorene stared at him. "Why do you want to do that?"

The stone prince looked down at his feet with an embarrassed expression. "Um, well, actually, I'm lost. And you seem to know your way around down here." He glanced hopefully at Cimorene's face, then sighed. "I suppose I can just wander around some more. I'll have to find a way out eventually."

"You'll run into a dragon and get eaten."

"I don't think it will hurt stone," the prince said. He sounded almost cheerful, as if he had only just realized that being made of stone might have some advantages.

"Maybe not, but you're sure to give the dragon indigestion," Cimorene said. "Bother! I don't have time for this!"

"I could wait here if you're coming back this way," the stone prince suggested.

Cimorene brightened, then frowned and shook her head. "No, one of the dragons might need to get into the Caves of Fire and Night, or it might be the turn of those dratted wizards. You can't stay here."

"Then—"

"I know! You can wait in the serving room, just off the banquet hall," Cimorene said. "It's close, there's plenty of room, and I know no one's using it today because I checked the schedule for Alianora yesterday. I can take a shortcut out the back to get to Roxim's without losing any *more* time. Come on."

"I really appreciate this," the stone prince said as they started off. "You don't know what it's like, being lost in the dark in these caves."

"How did it happen?" Cimorene asked.

The stone prince's expression became gloomy once more. "It's all that soothsayer's fault," he said.

"Soothsayer?"

"My father didn't think it was appropriate to invite fairies to a prince's christening, so he invited a soothsayer instead," the prince replied.

"The soothsayer took one look at me and said that I would grow up to do a great service for a king. I've been stuck with his blasted prophecy ever since."

"It doesn't sound so terrible to me," Cimorene said.

"It wasn't, at first," the stone prince admitted. "I had special tutors in all sorts of interesting things to prepare me for being of great service to a king. My father even sent me to a special school for people who're supposed to do special things."

"Did you do well?"

"I was top of my class," the stone prince said with a flash of pride. His face fell again. "That's part of the problem."

"I don't understand," Cimorene said. "This way. And can you walk a little faster, please? I'm in a hurry."

"It's been three years since I graduated, and everyone's still waiting for me to do something spectacular," the stone prince said, lengthening his stride. "The rest of my classmates are already making names for themselves. George started killing dragons right away, and Art went straight home and pulled some sort of magic sword out of a rock. Even the ones nobody expected to amount to much have done something. All Jack wanted to do was go back to his mother's farm and raise beans, and he ended up stealing a magic harp and killing a giant and all sorts of things. I'm the only one who hasn't succeeded."

"Why not?"

The stone prince sighed again. "I don't know. At first it seemed as if I wouldn't have any trouble finding a king to serve. Every time there was a war, both kings asked me to lead their armies, and every king for miles around who'd lost his throne to a usurper sent a messenger to my father's court. It should have been simple. Only they were always so worried about whether I was going to side with their enemies that it was easier not to pick anyone."

"I see," said Cimorene. Privately she thought that the stone prince had been rather wishy-washy.

Some of her opinion must have crept into her tone because the stone prince nodded glumly. "You're right. It was a mistake As long as I didn't pick a king to serve, all the messengers and ambassadors and envoys stayed, hoping to persuade me. The inns around the castle were stuffed with them. It got to the point where I couldn't show my face without at least three of them pouncing on me.

"Finally I couldn't stand it any more, and I ran away. It was a relief at first, not having everyone hovering over me waiting for me to do something great. But after a while I started feeling uncomfortable. Then I realized that even if nobody around me expected me to do anything special in the service of a king, *I* expected me to do something.

"I was so flustered that I ran up to the next palace I saw and asked whether the king needed any services done. It turned out that he was ill, and his doctors had told him that the only thing that would cure him was a drink of the Water of Healing from the Caves of Fire and Night. So I left to get it at once."

"So that's what you were doing!" Cimorene said.

The stone prince gave her another gloomy nod. "I should have known better. That king had three sons, and the first two had already gone off to get the water and failed. Anyone with sense would have seen that the youngest son was the one who would succeed; it sticks out all over. But I was too eager to do my great service and get it over with, and I didn't stop and think."

"What happened?"

"It took me a long time to find the Caves of Fire and Night, but once I did, it wasn't hard to find the Water of Healing. The chamber's getting crowded. All the princes who've tried to get the water and failed have been turned into slabs of rock."

"I know. I've seen them," Cimorene said. "Watch out for your head; the ceiling is low along here."

"Then you know what it's like, and you've seen the two dippers on the wall by the spring." The stone prince's shoulders sagged. "I *knew* I should use the tin one. It was one of the first things we learned at school. But I thought it wouldn't do any harm if I just *looked* at the gold one, so I took it off the wall. And as soon as I touched it, I started to stiffen up."

"Um," said Cimorene. The stone prince was obviously well aware of how foolishly he had behaved. She saw no reason to make him feel worse by pointing it out to him again.

"So I stuck my arm in the spring," the prince said.

"You stuck your arm – oh, I see! That was clever," Cimorene said.

"Do you really think so?" the stone prince asked anxiously. "I thought that since the water from the spring is going to turn all the slabs of stone back into princes when someone finally succeeds in the quest, then the water ought to keep me from turning into a slab of stone in the first place. Only it didn't work the way I expected," he finished disconsolately.

"I can see that," Cimorene said. "But at least you can still do things. It would be much worse to have to lie there waiting for the right prince to come along and break the spell."

"I wouldn't have had to lie there very long," the stone prince said. "That king's youngest son is going to arrive any day now, I just know it. Anyway, if I were a slab of stone, I wouldn't know about it until it was all over and I'd been turned back into a prince again."

"How do you know?" Cimorene demanded. "Have you ever *been* a stone slab?"

The stone prince looked startled. "No, I haven't. I never thought of that."

"Well, start thinking now," Cimorene said tartly. "Here's the service room. Wait here for me, and don't go wandering off if I'm late getting back. I don't know how long this errand is going to take, and it would be very awkward for me if the dragons found you roaming through their tunnels."

"I'll remember," the stone prince promised. "But what do I do if someone comes in?"

"Duck into the banquet area," Cimorene said, showing him. "And if someone comes in there, too, curl up in the corner and pretend you're a rock."

"All right," the prince said doubtfully.

Cimorene did not like leaving him, but she

was even less enthusiastic about taking him to see Roxim. Roxim probably wouldn't object to the prince himself, though Cimorene suspected that there might have been some difficulty over his proposed theft of the Water of Healing. But explaining everything to the gray-green dragon would take hours. Roxim was nice, but he tended to take a simple view of things, and the prince's situation was anything but simple. So Cimorene gave the prince one more warning, just to make sure he understood, and started off toward Roxim's cave to finish her errand.

CHAPTER 12

*In Which Cimorene Calls on a Dragon,
and the Stone Prince Discovers a Plot*

The shortcut to Roxim's worked just as well as Cimorene had hoped, and she even made up some of the time she had lost earlier. Roxim was in, too. She could hear the scraping of his scales as he moved around inside. She stepped up to the entrance of the cave and called, "Dragon Roxim!"

Something round and shiny flew through the air, missing Cimorene by inches. It hit the wall of the tunnel with a loud clang and slid rattling to the floor. Cimorene jumped.

"Roxim!" she shouted at the top of her lungs.

"What's this?" the dragon said, poking his nose out of the cave entrance.

"I am Cimorene, princess to the dragon Kazul, and I offer you greetings and good fortune in all your endeavors." Cimorene thought it best to be particularly polite, in case Roxim were in a bad mood. She suspected he might be. In her experience, someone in a good mood did not throw things at visitors.

"Very good," Roxim said. "Nice to see you again and all that, but I haven't got time for visitors at the moment. Sorry."

"I'm not a visitor, exactly. Kazul sent me with a message for you."

"Oh, well, that's different. Just hand me that shield there, would you?"

Cimorene picked up the shield from the floor of the tunnel. There was a large dent in one side where it had hit the tunnel wall, and several smaller ones over the rest of it from banging against things on its way to the tunnel floor.

"You ought to be more careful," she said severely. "Just look at this!"

"Ha!" Roxim snorted, examining the dents. "Shoddy work, shoddy work, that's the problem. In my day, you could roll a knight in full armor down the far side of the Vanishing Mountain and bounce him off two or three cliffs without so much as scratching his surface, much less denting it. This cheap modern stuff just doesn't hold up."

"If you know it doesn't hold up, you shouldn't throw it around like that," Cimorene said. "You almost hit me."

Roxim shifted uncomfortably. "Sorry. Didn't mean anything by it."

"All right, but next time look before you throw things," Cimorene said, handing him the shield.

"I always have this problem when I try to find something," Roxim confided. "Never know where to look. Gets frustrating, and next thing you know I'm pitching armor at the walls. Bad habit, but hard to break."

"Maybe I could help," Cimorene suggested. "After I give you Kazul's message, that is."

"Don't need help to put dents in things," Roxim said. "Come to that, I don't really want it."

"I didn't mean help throw things," Cimorene said patiently. "I meant help find whatever you're looking for."

"Oh, that. Well, come in then."

Cimorene followed the dragon into a moderately large cave, similar to the one Kazul used as a living area. Roxim's cave, however, was full of clutter. Cimorene had to pick her way past bits of armor, one half of a pair of bookends, a box of tea, a pink scroll, three mismatched kitchen pots, a small wooden statue, a broken flute, and four partially burned candles. Roxim walked straight over the mess as if it weren't there, squashing a mangy-looking stuffed pigeon and flattening a tin cup in passing. He dropped the shield on a pile of silk flowers and waved Cimorene to a seat on a large wooden chest near one wall. "Now, what's this message of Kazul's?"

"It's about the wizards," Cimorene said, settling gingerly onto the dusty surface of the chest. She made a mental note to find Roxim a nice princess as soon as she possibly could. "Alianora and I found one of them picking dragonsbane a few days ago, and Kazul thinks King Tokoz will listen to you if you tell him about it."

"So that's where they got it," Roxim said in tones of disgust. "Pity you didn't mention it sooner."

Cimorene got a sinking feeling. "What do you mean?"

"Somebody poisoned King Tokoz this morning," Roxim explained. "Slipped some dragonsbane in his coffee. Fast-acting; nothing to be done. Now we need a new king."

"That's awful!" Cimorene said. "Do you know who did it?"

"Those dratted wizards, that's who," Roxim said angrily. "It's obvious. Stupid thing to do;

has to be wizards, by George! But Woraug won't listen to me."

"Woraug? What's Woraug got to do with it?"

"He's in charge of the investigation," Roxim replied. "Taking his time about it, too, if you ask me."

"But if the King was only poisoned this morning . . ."

"What does that have to do with it?" Roxim said unreasonably. "Besides, if Woraug doesn't hurry, he won't have the culprit in hand by the time the trials start tomorrow."

"Trials? You mean with Colin's Stone, to choose the new king?" Cimorene said with some hesitation. She did not see how it could be a trial for the person who had killed the King if they hadn't caught him yet, but she was not completely certain that the dragons didn't have some way of getting around the problem and trying him anyway.

"That's it," Roxim said, pleased. "And before I leave I have to find that emerald I picked up fifty years ago. Coronation present for the new King."

"But you haven't got a new King yet," Cimorene said, feeling somewhat bewildered. "And what if *you're* the King?"

Roxim smiled broadly. "Knew you were a nice gal. Me, the King! I rather like the idea. I still have to find the emerald, though. Wouldn't do to show up at the trials without a coronation present. Rum thing to do. Overconfident."

Though she was upset and more than a little worried, Cimorene helped Roxim as best she could. After about an hour of poking through the clutter, Cimorene found the emerald, wrapped in a gold-embroidered handkerchief and stuffed into the mouth of a large brass horn. Roxim thanked her and invited her to stay to tea, but Cimorene politely declined. She was eager to get back to Kazul, to tell her what had happened and decide what to do next.

Cimorene hurried back to Kazul's cave by the shortest route, thinking so hard about Tokoz's death that she forgot everything else. She found Kazul sleeping and was forced to wake her, despite her worries about the dragon's health. She knew Kazul would want to hear about the King of the Dragons as soon as possible, and she wanted to hear what Kazul made of Woraug's involvement in the investigation.

"Back already?" Kazul said, opening her eyes. "Didn't Roxim get you in to see King Tokoz?"

"No," Cimorene said. She hesitated, uncertain of the best way to break the news. "It was too late."

"Too late?" Kazul raised her head, startled.

She eyed Cimorene briefly, then said. "All right, let's have it. What's happened?"

"King Tokoz was poisoned this morning. Roxim said someone put dragonsbane in his coffee."

Kazul snorted. "Somebody who knew Tokoz pretty well." Seeing Cimorene's surprised expression, she explained, "Tokoz drank Turkish coffee every morning. The stuff is strong enough to take the roof off your mouth. It's why no one ever went to talk to him over breakfast. You could boil a whole field's worth of dragonsbane in Turkish coffee without changing the taste enough to notice. Or the texture."

Cimorene tried to imagine coffee, even Turkish coffee, strong enough to take the roof off a dragon's mouth and failed. "I told Roxim about the wizard Alianora and I met, and Roxim said I ought to tell Woraug because Woraug is in charge of finding the poisoner," she said. "But—"

"But when you caught Antorell picking dragonsbane, he thought Woraug had sent you," Kazul said. "If Woraug's mixed up with wizards—" She broke off, coughing. Cimorene watched her anxiously, but the coughing spasm did not last long. "I don't like this," Kazul finished when she got her breath back.

"I don't, either," Cimorene agreed. "But what can we do about it?"

Kazul frowned and said nothing. For several minutes, the two sat and thought in silence. Then Kazul said, "We can't do anything until the new King has been chosen. Did Roxim say when the testing will be?"

"Tomorrow," Cimorene said.

"Tomorrow!" Kazul surged to her feet. "Why didn't you say so at once? If I'm to be at the Ford of Whispering Snakes tomorrow, I have to—"

"Lie down!" Cimorene commanded. Kazul looked at her in surprise and collapsed in another fit of coughing. Cimorene waited until the dragon's coughing had subsided, then said sternly, "You're in no condition to go hauling rocks all over the countryside. I'd be surprised if you can even fly as far as the end of the pass. I think you're going to have to give up on the trials this time around."

Kazul made a choking noise. Cimorene looked at her in alarm, then realized that the dragon was laughing.

"It's not optional, Princess," Kazul said. "All the adult dragons in the Mountains of Morning are required to show up, no matter what condition they're in."

"But—"

"There is *no* acceptable excuse for missing the testing of a new King," Kazul repeated. "None.

And I have a great deal to do before I leave, so if you'll—"

"If anything needs to be done around here, I'll do it," Cimorene said firmly. "If you don't rest, you won't be able to fly at all, and then how will you get to the ford?"

"A reasonable point," Kazul said, settling reluctantly back into place. "Very well. The first thing I need is a coronation present for the new King. There's a jeweled helmet on a shelf in the second storeroom that might do. Bring it out so I can take a look at it."

Cimorene spent the rest of the evening running errands for Kazul. Besides choosing a coronation gift (Kazul rejected the helmet and two crowns before deciding on a scepter made of gold and crystal), innumerable messages had to be delivered to various dragons who were in charge of arranging the trials. This one had to be informed of Kazul's ill health, so that it could be taken into account when the order of the testing was established; that one had to be told that Kazul would not be able to join the coronation procession. Substitutes had to be found to perform Kazul's various ceremonial duties, then their names had to be approved by a surly dragon in charge of protocol, and finally the substitutions had to be recorded on all the lists of all the dragons who were managing each of the events. It reminded Cimorene strongly of Linderwall and her parents' court.

By the time the last arrangement had been made and the last message delivered, it was very late and Cimorene was exhausted. She was also very glad she had not let Kazul do all the running around. The dragon, who had slept most of the time Cimorene was out, was looking much better, even in the dim light of Cimorene's lamp. Tired but satisfied, Cimorene went to her room and dropped into bed.

Cimorene was up early the next morning, stirring a dozen ostrich eggs in a large iron kettle for Kazul's breakfast. Kazul ate all of them, then slid out of the cave and prepared to leave for the Ford of Whispering Snakes.

"Don't fret, Princess," Kazul said. "The testing doesn't start until ten. I have plenty of time to get there, even if I stop to rest now and then." Her voice sounded much better than it had the day before, and it no longer seemed to rasp her throat. "While I'm gone, why don't you visit Woraug's princess? See if she's noticed anything odd these past few days. We need to know as much as we can before we talk to the new King about Woraug and the wizards."

"All right," Cimorene said. "As soon as I'm done with the dishes."

Kazul turned and leaped into the air, her wings churning clouds of dust from the dry surface of the ground. Cimorene squinted after her and shouted, "Good luck!" Kazul's wings dipped in answer before the dragon soared out of sight behind the shoulder of the next mountain. Cimorene stood looking after Kazul, her forehead wrinkling in worry. After a moment she shook herself and went inside. She had work to do.

Washing the dishes did not take long, and as soon as she was done, Cimorene set off to visit Alianora. The tunnels and passageways were silent and empty, and Cimorene's footsteps echoed eerily through the darkness. She began to wish she had taken the longer route along the outside of the mountain. She had not realized that the dragon city would seem so strange and lifeless with all the dragons gone.

"Psst! Cimorene!"

Cimorene jumped. She whirled in the direction of the voice, raising her lamp like a club, and Alianora stepped out of the adjoining tunnel and into the circle of light. In one hand she clutched a large bucket, three-quarters full of soapy water, and she looked rather pale.

"Alianora!" Cimorene said, lowering her arm. "What are you doing out here?"

"Shhh!" Alianora said. She looked nervously

over her shoulder. "Woraug told me to scrub off the table in the banquet room while everyone was away. And – and I heard someone moving around in there. Even though everyone but us is gone. And I dropped my lamp, and—"

"Oh, my goodness," Cimorene said. "The stone prince! I'd forgotten all about him."

"Who?"

"The stone prince." Quickly, Cimorene explained how she had found and hidden him the day before. "And I hadn't thought about it until now, but this is the perfect time to get him out of the mountains," she finished. "All the dragons are gone and no one will see him. Come on, before I forget again."

Alianora nodded dubiously, and the two girls headed for the banquet room. When they arrived, Cimorene went in first, holding her lamp high. "Prince?" she called. "Are you there? It's me, Cimorene."

"Yes, I'm here," said the stone prince, unfolding stiffly from a gray lump in the corner. "I'm glad you're back. Who's this you've brought with you?"

"Princess Alianora of the Duchy of Toure-on-Marsh," Cimorene said. "She's the princess of the dragon Woraug just now."

"Does her father need a great service done for him?" the prince asked hopefully.

"Not that I know of," Cimorene replied. "Unless you're good at getting rid of aunts, but that would be more of a service to Alianora than to her father."

"I can think of nothing that would make me happier," the prince said with evident admiration as he bowed stiffly to Alianora. "Good afternoon, Princess. Or should it be 'good evening'? It's hard to tell without windows."

Alianora blushed and looked down at her bucket without answering.

"Actually, it's good morning," Cimorene told the prince. "I'm sorry it took me so long to come back for you, but . . . well, a lot has been going on."

Alianora looked up sharply. "You've been sitting here in the dark all *night?*" She shuddered. "You could at least have left him a candle, Cimorene."

"Thank you for the thought, Princess Alianora, but it's just as well she didn't," the stone prince said. "If I'd been sitting here with a lit candle, they'd have noticed me right away. And an unlit candle isn't much use in the dark, is it?"

"What do you mean?" Cimorene said. "Who would have noticed you?"

"The dragon and the two men he was talking to," replied the prince. "I think they were wizards."

"What?" said Cimorene and Alianora together.

"Well, they talked as if they were wizards," the prince said. "They weren't carrying staffs, though."

"What did they look like?" Cimorene said.

"They were both tall, and they both had beards. The older one's was gray and the younger one's was brown."

"Antorell and Zemenar!" Cimorene said. "And they were talking to a dragon?"

The stone prince nodded.

"Then they wouldn't have been carrying staffs. Dragons are allergic to them. Did you hear what they said?"

"Something about a contest," the stone prince said. "The wizards were going to fix it so this dragon would win. It sounded like a kind of cross-country race, and the wizards were going to hide along the path and — and help the dragon out somehow. I'm afraid I'm not very clear about that part. Spells aren't my specialty. I'm much better at hopeless causes."

Alianora and Cimorene exchanged appalled glances.

"The trials with Colin's Stone to pick the new King!" Alianora said.

"Which dragon?" Cimorene asked urgently. "Do you know which dragon they were talking to?"

"I only heard the name once," the prince said. He sounded apologetic and a little embarrassed. "And I don't think I got it right. It's too silly."

"Tell us!" Cimorene commanded.

"Well, it *sounded* like 'warthog,'" the prince said in an even more apologetic tone than before.

"Could it have been Woraug?" Cimorene asked.

"That's it!" the prince said. "I knew it couldn't *really* have been warthog."

"What a pity you remembered," said a voice from the entrance into the banquet hall.

Cimorene whirled. Antorell stood in the doorway, staff in hand, watching them with an intolerably smug expression.

CHAPTER 13

*In Which Alianora Discovers an
Unexpected Use for Soap and Water, and
Cimorene Has Difficulty with a Dragon*

Antorell looked past Cimorene and Alianora as if they were not there and spoke directly to the stone prince. "I told Father someone was listening. He won't be happy when he finds out I was right, but he'll feel better when I tell him I've taken care of things. He might even let me have the first look in the King's Crystal, once Woraug gives it to us."

"So that's what you're after!" Cimorene said.

Antorell favored her with a superior smile. "Quite right, Princess Cimorene. The King's Crystal will show us the whereabouts of every piece of useful and interesting magic in the world. All we'll have to do is go out and pick them up."

"Somehow I don't think it will be that easy," Cimorene murmured.

"We knew Tokoz would never give it to us, but Woraug will, as soon as he's King of the Dragons. He'll have to, or we'll tell everyone how we were the ones who made sure *he* was the new king. Of course, we can't afford to have anybody around who might make . . . awkward revelations. I doubt that dragons will listen to a couple of hysterical princesses, but he" – Antorell pointed at the stone prince – "will have to go."

"What are you going to do?" Alianora demanded. She was plainly frightened, and Cimorene could see that her knuckles were white with the force of her grip on the handle of the scrub bucket.

"Oh, gravel seems appropriate, don't you think?" Antorell said. "No one will notice a few more rocks around here."

"Ought I to be taking this person seriously?" the stone prince said in a rather doubtful tone.

"You'd better if you don't want to end up as a lot of little pebbles," Aliancra answered. She still sounded frightened, but she seemed to be getting a grip on herself. "He's a wizard."

"You wouldn't be talking about gravel if *you*

were the one who had to sweep the floor," Cimorene said to Antorell. She stepped forward as she spoke, hoping to get between Antorell and the stone prince before Antorell noticed what she was doing. She didn't think Antorell was a good enough wizard to do any real harm, but there was no point in taking chances.

"Stay where you are, Princess Cimorene," Antorell commanded. "I'll deal with you in a moment."

"Must you be so theatrical?" Cimorene said.

"Theatrical? You think I'm being *theatrical?*" Antorell said furiously. "I am simply showing a proper respect for the importance of this moment!"

"You're showing off," Cimorene said flatly. "And you're not doing it very well."

"He doesn't sound much like a wizard to me," the stone prince said. "Is he always like this?"

"Enough!" Antorell cried, and raised his staff. Light shimmered along its length and began to gather at the lower end. Grinning wolfishly, the wizard tilted the staff, aiming it toward the stone prince.

"Stop that!" Alianora said. Antorell ignored her. "I said, *stop it!*" Alianora shouted, and threw her bucket at Antorell's head.

Alianora's aim was off. The bucket hit

Antorell's shoulder. A bolt of fire shot from the end of his staff and whizzed between Cimorene and the stone prince to strike the far wall with a whumping noise and a shower of sparks. Antorell staggered, slipped in the cascade of soapy water, and fell over the bucket, dropping his staff in the process.

Cimorene darted in and kicked Antorell's staff out of his reach. He stared up at her from a mound of soggy silk and soapsuds. "You can't *do* this to me!" he shrieked.

Something in his voice made Cimorene and her friends look at him more closely. Alianora's eyes went wide, and Cimorene blinked in surprise. "He's – he's collapsing," Alianora said in a stunned voice.

"He's melting," Cimorene corrected her.

"I can't be melting!" Antorell cried. "I'm a *wizard!* It's not fa—" His head disappeared into a small brown puddle, and his cries stopped.

There was a moment of astonished silence. "I thought it was witches who melt when you dump water over them," the stone prince said at last.

"It is, usually," Cimorene said. "What on earth did you put in that bucket, Alianora?"

"Just water and soap, and a little lemon juice to make it smell nicer," Alianora said.

"Um," said Cimorene, thinking hard. "I'll bet

there's a simpler way of melting wizards, but we don't have time right now to figure out what it is. How many buckets can you get hold of in a hurry?"

"Buckets?" Alianora said. "Two, counting this one. And I suppose I could borrow one from Hallanna; that's three."

"And I've got two in the kitchen, and I expect the iron kettle is big enough. That's six altogether; two for each of us. You will help, won't you?" Cimorene added, turning to the stone prince.

"Of course," the prince assured her. "Help with what?"

"Stopping those wizards," Cimorene said. "We can't let them make Woraug the next King of the Dragons by trickery."

"I don't see how we can stop them," Alianora said. "We can't possibly get to the Ford of Whispering Snakes before the trials start, and even if we could, we don't know where the wizards will be hiding."

"If we tell the dragons that Woraug's trying to cheat, they'll stop the trials," Cimorene said with more confidence than she felt. "That will give us time to find the wizards. And I've got a way to get us to the ford. You go start collecting buckets. I'll meet you at your place after I get the things I'll need from Kazul's."

"What about . . ." Alianora gestured with distaste at the wet, messy lump of robes in the center of the puddle that was all that remained of Antorell.

"We'll clean it up when we get back," Cimorene said. "This is more important."

Alianora nodded, and the three left the banquet room. The stone prince decided to accompany Alianora since he was not a fast walker and Cimorene had farther to go. Cimorene left them when they reached the main tunnel and ran back to Kazul's cave. There she went straight to her room and opened the drawer where she kept odds and ends. In the back left-hand corner, carefully wrapped in a handkerchief, were the three black feathers she had taken from beneath the left wing of the bird she had killed in the Enchanted Forest. She shoved the whole packet into her pocket without bothering to unwrap it and went on to the kitchen to collect her buckets. Then she hurried through the tunnels to Woraug's cave, where Alianora and the stone prince were waiting.

When Cimorene arrived, she found the stone prince pumping water to fill Alianora's third bucket while Alianora mixed soap and lemon juice into the second. Cimorene set her pots and pails next to the pump and went to help Alianora.

"Now what?" Alianora said when all the buckets were full of cleaning mixture.

Cimorene reached into her pocket and dug out the package. Gently, she unfolded the handkerchief and removed one of the feathers, noticing as she did that the package also contained the pebble she had picked up in the Caves of Fire and Night. "If we each take two buckets, can we still link elbows without spilling too much?" she asked.

Alianora and the stone prince looked at each other, shrugged, and picked up two buckets each. Cimorene took the last bucket and the iron pot, holding the handle of the pot with only three fingers so that she could keep a grip on the feather with her thumb and forefinger. A series of awkward maneuvers followed as Alianora and the stone prince tried to link elbows with Cimorene without losing their balance or dropping one of their buckets. In the process, Cimorene's skirt got soaked.

"It's a good thing I'm not a wizard," Cimorene said. "Ready? Here we go." She twisted her hand toward the edge of the iron pot and let go of the black feather. "I wish we were at the Ford of Whispering Snakes," she said as the feather fell, and the room dissolved around them.

They materialized at the very edge of a river,

on a flat, narrow rock that jutted out over the water, and Alianora immediately slipped on the wet stone. If the stone prince had not been so solid and heavy, all three of them would have fallen into the river. As it was, it took Cimorene and Alianora several seconds to regain their balance. When she was finally sure of her footing, Cimorene breathed a sigh of relief and quickly looked about her.

The Ford of Whispering Snakes was crowded. Dragons of all sizes and shades of green lined the banks of the river and filled the spaces beneath the towering trees of the Enchanted Forest. On the far bank, a pale dragon was poring over a parchment list that Cimorene thought she remembered seeing during one of the many errands she had run the previous night. All the dragons seemed to be talking at once, and none of them noticed Cimorene and her friends.

"Hello, dragons!" Cimorene shouted, trying to make herself heard above the noise.

"Here, now! What's all this?" an olive-green dragon on the bank demanded, turning. "Someone's trying to sneak a look at the trials."

"S-s-s-sneaksssss," hissed a soft but nonetheless clearly audible voice from somewhere near Cimorene's feet. Cimorene jumped and looked down, but though she craned her neck to see all around her, she could not find the second speaker.

"Get rid of them before Troum comes back with Colin's Stone," another dragon advised.

"We aren't trying to sneak in, and we don't care about watching the trials," Cimorene said, wishing she dared to look around for Kazul. "We came to warn you about the wizards."

"Wiz-z-zardssss," the soft voice echoed.

"Wizards?" the olive-green dragon said skeptically. "There aren't any wizards here."

"No, but they've figured out some way of interfering with your choice of the next king," Cimorene said. "They're hiding somewhere. You have to put off the trials with Colin's Stone until we can find them and stop them. If you'll just tell Kazul we're here—"

"Put off the trials?" the olive-green dragon interrupted. "Impossible! They've been under way for half an hour. We can't just stop in the middle. Who are all you people, anyway?"

A flicker of motion caught Cimorene's eye, and she looked down just in time to see a thin red snake dart from one clump of weeds to the next. "S-s-s-sneaksss," whispered the soft voice an instant later. "S-s-sneaksss and wiz-z-zardsss."

"I wasn't asking you," the dragon said severely in the general direction of the snake.

"And whatever they are, they certainly aren't wizards."

"They look like somebody's princesses to me," a blue-green dragon said. "Pity, that. It would be so much simpler to eat them and get them out of the way."

"Are you sure?" said a third dragon. "The one on the end doesn't look like a princess."

"I'm beginning to think this wasn't such a good idea," the stone prince said.

"He may not be a princess, but he doesn't look edible, either," the blue-green dragon pointed out. "And these other two are definitely princesses. You can't go eating them out of hand."

"Princessessss," hissed the voice from under the rock.

"Oh, princesses," the olive-green dragon said. "No wonder they're so full of wild tales."

"It's true!" Cimorene said desperately. "If you don't believe us, take us to Kazul; she will."

"I can't do that!" the olive-green dragon said, shocked. "Kazul's third in line now, after Mazarin and Woraug. You can't talk to people who are that close to making their attempt with the stone. It would distract them."

"Woraug!" Alianora said. "Woraug's next in line?"

"Yes, he should be starting off any minute now," said the olive-green dragon. "Then comes Mazarin, and then Kazul. I don't expect it will take long, though. Nobody's carried the stone for more than a mile or two yet."

"But I'm Kazul's princess!" Cimorene said.

"I don't care who you are," the dragon replied crossly. "You can't talk to Kazul until she's done with her turn."

"That will be too late!" Cimorene cried. "You don't understand. Woraug and the wizards—"

"I've had enough of your wizards," the olive-green dragon said. "You're a confounded nuisance, and you ought not to be pushing your way in here where you're not wanted. Go away!"

"Cimorene, what are we going to do?" Alianora said as the olive-green dragon turned and stalked determinedly away.

"At hero's school we were always taught that if you couldn't persuade anyone to help you with something, it meant that you were supposed to do it by yourself," the stone prince said diffidently. "And we *are* prepared." He lifted one of his buckets slightly.

"But we don't know where the wizards are," Alianora said. "We have to find them before we can stop them, and there isn't time."

"S-s-stop the wiz-z-ardsss," whispered the soft voice.

"That's the first sensible thing you've said since we got here," Cimorene said to the hissing whisper.

"Can't you just wish to be where the wizards are?" the stone prince asked Cimorene.

"No, you have to know where you're going, or the spell doesn't work," Cimorene said.

For a moment all three were glumly silent. Cimorene stared at the water, remembering how and where she had got the feathers. Suddenly she raised her head.

"We may not know where the wizards are, but I'll bet I know someone who can find out. Hold this for a minute."

Cimorene handed one of her buckets to Alianora, then dug out the packet of feathers. She pulled the second feather from the packet and grabbed Alianora's elbow. "Hold tight, everybody. I wish we were at Morwen's house," Cimorene said, and dropped the feather.

The scenery shifted abruptly, and they were standing on Morwen's porch. The house was just as tidy-looking as Cimorene remembered, and the porch floor gleamed as if it had just been washed. A black and white cat, startled by their sudden appearance, fell off the porch railing. Four others left off washing themselves to stare at Cimorene with unwinking green and yellow eyes.

"I need to talk to Morwen," Cimorene said to the cats. "It's an emergency."

A lean tiger-striped cat rose and oozed through a crack in the door. Cimorene unwound herself from Alianora and the stone prince and set her bucket on the porch floor. "I hope this works," she muttered to herself as Alianora and the prince placed their buckets beside hers.

CᕼᗩᑭTEᖇ 14

*In Which the Wizards Try to Make Trouble,
and Cimorene Does Something about It*

The door of the cottage opened and Morwen stepped out. "What sort of emergency?" she asked. She studied Alianora and the stone prince for a moment, then peered at Cimorene over the tops of her glasses and added with some severity, "I hope you weren't referring to *his* predicament. He may well find it an inconvenience, but it certainly isn't an emergency. Not by my standards, anyway."

"No," said Cimorene, "I was talking about the wizards. They've poisoned the King of the Dragons, and now they're trying to interfere with Colin's Stone so that Woraug will be the new king. We have to stop them, but we don't know where they are, and Woraug's going to try to carry the stone any minute. Can you find them for us?"

Morwen blinked twice and shoved her glasses back into place with her forefinger. "I see," she said. "You're right. It's an emergency. I'll do what I can. But if you don't tell me the whole story later, when there's a bit more time, I shall – I shall turn you all into mice and give you to the cats. Wait here."

As she spoke, Morwen disappeared into the house. She reappeared a moment later, holding a small mirror and muttering over it. "Colin's Stone," she said, and breathed on the glass. She looked up. "Any wizard in particular?"

"Zemenar, the Head Wizard of the Society of Wizards," Cimorene said, wishing Morwen would go faster and knowing she couldn't.

"I should have guessed," Morwen said. She turned back to the mirror. "Zemenar," she said, and breathed on the glass once more. Then she motioned to Cimorene to come and look.

Cimorene obeyed, and Alianora and the stone prince crowded closely behind her. The mirror showed a blurry, wavering picture of the Ford of Whispering Snakes. As Cimorene watched, the picture moved slowly along one bank of the river, past the waiting dragons and the immense trees of the Enchanted Forest and on down the river.

"Can't it go any faster?" Alianora whispered.

"There's no need to whisper, and no, it can't," Morwen said. "Not if you want to be sure of finding these wizards of yours on the first try, and it doesn't sound as if you have time to waste on mistakes."

The picture in the mirror continued to creep along the bank. Cimorene pulled the third and last feather out of her pocket and brushed it nervously across her fingers while she waited.

"What's that?" the stone prince said suddenly.

The mirror-picture stopped, then moved up the bank, away from the river toward a thicket of blackberry brambles. Cimorene saw the tip of a wooden staff poking up above the thicket. Tensely, she waited for the mirror to show the far side of the brambles.

"It's them!" Alianora said. She sounded frightened and excited at the same time. "Oh, dear!"

Cimorene took a good look at the picture in the mirror. Five wizards were standing in an opening behind the blackberry thicket, leaning on their staffs and looking at the sky. Suddenly, one of the wizards pointed. The others peered upward, nodded, and raised their staffs.

"Get the buckets!" Cimorene said. Cats scattered in all directions as the stone prince pounded across the porch behind Cimorene and Alianora. "Hang on; here we go. I wish—"

"Not without me you—" Morwen said, grabbing Cimorene's shoulder.

"—we were at the blackberry thicket where the wizards are," Cimorene said, and dropped the feather.

"—don't," Morwen finished as the porch winked out and was replaced by blackberries.

The five wizards were standing in an arc just in front of the bramble. Each of them held his staff so that the lower end was about a foot above the ground, pointing at something hidden in the moss at their feet. An unpleasant yellow-green light dripped from the ends of the staffs, and the moss where the wizards were standing was brown and dead. The wizards' backs were toward Cimorene and her friends.

"Now!" Cimorene cried. As the wizards began to turn, she set one of her buckets on the ground and lifted the other in both hands. Taking careful aim, she flung the soapy water over a black-haired wizard in the center of the arc.

"Charge!" yelled the stone prince, and threw one of his buckets at the nearest wizard.

"Take that, you cheats!" said Alianora, dumping the first of her buckets over another.

"What – this is impossible!" said one of the wizards indignantly as he began to melt.

"Too bad," Cimorene said, throwing her second load of water at the next-to-last wizard.

"Watch where you're throwing that!" Morwen said to the stone prince, who had sloshed his second bucket over the fifth wizard with such enthusiasm that water sprayed in all directions.

"Sorry," the prince apologized. "Is that all of them?"

"It's all five of the ones we saw," Cimorene said cautiously.

"Then we did it!" Alianora said.

"Not quite," said Zemenar, stepping out of the bushes behind Morwen. "You interrupted the spell, of course, but we were nearly finished anyway. And as long as the stone remains enchanted, Woraug won't have any trouble getting it all the way to the Vanishing Mountain. Look." He pointed with his staff, and Cimorene saw three dragons, high in the air, flying steadily toward the mountains. One of them had a long black stone clutched in his claws, and the other two appeared to be escorting him at a careful distance.

"Woraug and the two judges," Cimorene murmured.

Zemenar nodded. "You might as well put that bucket down," he went on, turning to Alianora. "You can't throw it at me without melting your witch friend here. What's in it, by the way?"

"I don't see why we should tell you," Cimorene said as Alianora set the last of the six buckets down.

"Because I'm interested, Princess," Zemenar said with an oily smile. "And it will pass the time until the next shift gets here, and I can decide what to do with you."

"If you're interested, why don't you take a closer look?" said the stone prince, picking up Alianora's bucket.

"Stay where you are!" Zemenar commanded. As he spoke, he raised his staff and sidestepped so that Morwen was between him and the stone prince.

"If you insist," said the prince. He shrugged, lifted the bucket, and flung the water over Morwen and Zemenar at the same time.

"What — no!" Zemenar cried in horror as he began to melt. "Not soapsuds! It's demeaning."

"There's a little lemon juice in it, too," Alianora offered.

Zemenar glared at her. He was less than half his normal height and shrinking as they watched, while a dark puddle spread out beneath him. "Lemon juice! Bah! How dare you do such a thing? I'm the Head Wizard of the Society of Wizards!" His voice grew fainter and higher as he shrank. "Interfering busybodies! Soapsuds! Of all the undignified tricks. You'll be sorry for this! You can't melt a wizard forever, you know! You'll be sor . . ."

The wizard's voice ceased. All that remained of him was a pile of silk robes and a long wooden staff lying on some damp moss. Alianora and Cimorene stared for a moment, then Alianora turned to the stone prince.

"I'm glad he's gone," she said, "but how could you melt Morwen just to get at that wizard?"

"But I didn't," the stone prince said. "Look."

Cimorene and Alianora turned. Morwen seemed no shorter than usual, though she certainly looked very damp. She had taken off her glasses and was shaking water off them. "Don't just stand there," she said crossly to Cimorene. "Hand me a dry handkerchief."

"Just a minute," Cimorene said, checking her pockets. She found the handkerchief that had been wrapped around the magic feathers and handed it to Morwen. "Um, why *didn't* you melt?"

"Clean living," Morwen said as she began to dry her glasses on Cimorene's handkerchief.

"I thought as much," the stone prince said in a satisfied tone. "Nobody who lives in a house as clean as yours could possibly melt in a bucket of soapsuds."

"Quite right," Morwen said approvingly. "You have a good head on your shoulders, young man. What's this?" She held up a sharp-edged black pebble.

"It's a piece of stone I found in the Caves of Fire and Night," Cimorene said.

"Where, exactly?"

"In the King's Cave," Cimorene said. "Morwen, shouldn't we do something about that spell Zemenar mentioned?"

Alianora was watching the sky, shading her eyes with her hand. "Woraug's nearly halfway to the mountain," she said anxiously.

"Good," said Morwen, though neither Cimorene nor Alianora could tell which of them she was talking to. The witch shook her wet robes and walked over to the patch of dead moss where the wizards had been working, picking her way carefully past little piles of robes and staffs. Cimorene followed. In the center of the brown area was a black stone the size of Cimorene's fist. A web of yellow-green light flickered across its smooth surface.

"Sloppy," Morwen said. "Very sloppy. Though I'm not surprised. Wizards always seem to depend on brute force when a little subtlety would be far more effective." She fingered Cimorene's pebble for a moment, then reached out and dropped it on top of the wizards' stone.

There was a noise like a great deal of popcorn

all popping at once, and the light that flickered over the black stone spat yellow-green sparks in all directions. Alianora jumped and backed away. Cimorene would have liked to do the same, but she did not want to give Morwen a bad impression of her courage, so she stayed where she was.

The sparks died, and the flickering light went out. From the sky high above came a faint shriek of surprise and rage. Cimorene looked up and saw three black specks in the sky. No, not three: four, and the two escort dragons were swooping to catch the speck that was Colin's Stone, which Woraug had just dropped.

Cimorene gave a sigh of relief and looked at Morwen. "So much for Woraug and the wizards," she said. "We didn't even need the fireproofing spell. What did you do?"

"And what happens now?" Alianora added.

"Duck," said Morwen, and threw herself sideways into the bushes.

"Wha—" said the stone prince, and then he and Cimorene and Alianora were engulfed by a blast of dragon fire.

The stone prince leaped in front of the two princesses, but he was much too late to protect them. Fortunately the fireproofing spell was still in effect, and neither of them even felt warm, though Alianora lost the ends of her sleeves and Cimorene's hemline rose six scorched inches.

"I knew I shouldn't have said that about the fireproofing spell," Cimorene muttered.

With a wordless snarl and a thunder of wings, Woraug landed just in front of the little group.

"You!" he shouted when he saw Cimorene. "I might have known it would be you!" Flame shot from his mouth once more, but it was just as useless as it had been the first time.

Cimorene glanced up and saw one of the escort dragons spiraling down to see what was going on. "You might as well give up, Woraug," she said, hoping to distract the angry dragon long enough for help to arrive. "You can't be King of the Dragons now."

"I'll tear you limb from limb!" Woraug raged. "Every last one of you!" One arm shot out as he spoke, and shining silver claws snapped around the stone prince's waist.

Alianora screamed.

"Hurry *up!*" Cimorene shouted at the dragon in the sky.

The dragon heard and dove toward them, but he was not fast enough. Woraug shoved the stone prince into his mouth and bit down hard. An instant later he howled in pain and spat out the prince and four teeth.

"What *is* all this?" said the escort dragon,

landing carefully beside Woraug. The clearing was getting rather crowded.

"A plot to cheat on the test to see who the next King of the Dragons will be," Cimorene said. "Woraug was in it, and a lot of wizards."

"Are you all right?" Alianora asked the stone prince, who was just picking himself up. His stone was black in places from the dragon fire, but otherwise he seemed unhurt.

"More or less," the stone prince said. "But just look what that fire did to my clothes! And that dragon's put a chip in my sleeve. What am I supposed to do about that? It's not as if I can just change clothes when I get home, you know."

"That's ridiculous!" the escort dragon told Cimorene. "No dragon would cooperate with wizards. I don't see any wizards, either. I think you're making it up."

"Of course you don't see any wizards," Cimorene said, feeling very cross. "We melted them."

"Melted them?"

"Where do you think those staffs came from?" Cimorene pointed at the wizards' staffs lying across the scattered brown puddles.

The dragon backed up a pace and sniffed experimentally.

"It's all quite true," Morwen said, poking her

head out of the bushes. "And we'll be more than happy to explain the whole thing to your new King as soon as you have one. Provided, of course, that you take that maniac away before he burns the whole Enchanted Forest to the ground." She gestured at Woraug. "Cimorene, I really must insist on getting a copy of that fire-proofing spell. It will clearly be worth every minute of the months of hunting it will take me to find some hens' teeth, and I may as well get started as soon as I can."

"Who's that?" said the escort dragon. "Morwen? That does it! This is too much for me. I'm taking you all into custody until the trials are over and the King can sort it out. Come along."

"I assume that doesn't apply to me," Woraug rumbled. He winced as he spoke.

"It certainly does," the escort dragon said. "I said *all*, and I meant *all*. If I'd meant 'all the humans,' I'd have said 'all the humans,' or maybe 'some of you' or 'you over there' or 'all you non-dragons' or—"

"Nonsense!" Woraug interrupted. "Don't you know who I am?"

"You're the dragon who caused a ruckus just now for no reason I can see," the escort dragon replied. "And it's my duty and my job to take you into custody. When the trials are over, you

can explain it to the King, and if I've done something wrong, well, I'll take what I have coming.
And if I haven't, you'll take yours. And—"

"All right, all right," Woraug said. "But I warn
you, you'll regret this."

"That's as may be," the escort dragon said
with dignity. "Right now, though, you're in
custody along with the rest of these people, and
you'd better not go snacking on any of them
until things are sorted out. I saw what you did
to the gray one."

"Did you?" said the stone prince. "Then what
are you going to do about this chip in my
sleeve?"

"Tell it to the King," the escort dragon advised. "Now, off we go, the lot of you."

Morwen came cautiously out of the bushes,
brushing leaves from her already wet black
robes. She stopped and peered at the escort
dragon over the tops of her glasses. "This has
not been a good day for anyone's clothes," she
said severely. "I shall send the cleaning bill to
your king."

"Whatever you want," the escort dragon said
impatiently. "Come *on*."

Scowling furiously, Woraug marched off into
the forest. The stone prince and Alianora followed, talking in low voices. Morwen paused to
pick up the wizards' black rock and Cimorene's

pebble, then went on after them. Cimorene hesitated.

"Go on," said the escort dragon.

"I will, but I think you ought to know that another batch of wizards is supposed to show up soon," Cimorene said. "Zemenar said something about a second shift. I don't know what they can do without the stone they were using, but I'm sure they'll try something."

"Wizards always do," the escort dragon said with a sigh. He studied the wizards' staffs that were lying around the clearing with a melancholy air. "All right, I'll send someone back to keep an eye on things as soon as we get to the ford. Whatever was going on here, there certainly were wizards in it, and that's enough for me."

"Good," said Cimorene. "And thank you." She smiled at the startled expression on the dragon's face and started after the others.

CHAPTER 15

*In Which the Dragons Crown a New King,
and Cimorene Gets a New Job*

The walk to the Ford of Whispering Snakes took longer than Cimorene had expected. The trees of the Enchanted Forest grew close together in many places, forcing the dragons to take a zigzag path instead of heading straight up the bank of the river. Woraug, who was in the lead, seemed to be deliberately setting a slow pace. Cimorene was sure he was hoping that the second shift of wizards would arrive at the blackberry clearing before the dragons at the ford had been warned. She had no idea what would happen then, but she doubted that it would be good. The escort dragon was not interested in Cimorene's worries, however, and he refused to speed things up, so the group ambled on.

As they approached the ford at last, they heard cheering ahead of them. Woraug flinched visibly, and Alianora and the stone prince were startled out of their quiet conversation.

"What's that?" Alianora said.

"Sounds to me as if we have a new King," their escort said with great satisfaction. "That means I can get you lot off my hands right away. What a relief! I thought I was going to be stuck with you for hours."

Alianora looked faintly indignant at this unflattering opinion. Morwen was merely amused. Woraug's wings sagged momentarily, but then he seemed to pull himself back together, and he continued on as confidently as ever. Cimorene's concern deepened. What if Woraug managed to convince the new King that they were all lying?

They reached the edge of the cheering crowd of dragons. "Who did it?" the escort dragon asked. "Who's the new King?"

"How should I know?" the other responded. "I can't see a thing from way out here."

"You'll find out soon enough," the escort dragon said. Then he raised his voice and shouted, "Make way! Coming through! Prisoners for the King! Make way!"

The crowd of dragons parted reluctantly, and the escort dragon herded the group forward, still shouting. They made their way through the cheering dragons until they reached the edge of the river. "Stand away!" shouted someone in the crowd. "Stand away for the King!"

The nearby dragons drew back, leaving Woraug, the escort dragon, and Cimorene and her friends standing by themselves on the trampled moss. As the dragons moved away, Cimorene caught sight of Kazul, lying comfortably beside the river. "Kazul!" Cimorene cried, and ran forward. "Are you all right?"

A mottled dragon standing beside Kazul shifted and flicked his tail angrily at Cimorene. "You should say 'Your Majesty,'" he said with a warning scowl.

"Don't be ridiculous, Frax. She's my princess," Kazul said. "I'm quite all right, Cimorene. What are you doing here?"

"*You're* the new King of the Dragons?" Cimorene said in astonishment. "But – but when you left this morning, you could barely fly! How did you get Colin's Stone all the way from here to the Vanishing Mountain?"

"Colin's Stone apparently does more than merely pick out the right King," Kazul said. "The minute I picked it up, I felt fine."

"This is impossible!" Woraug said.

"Are you accusing me of fraud?" Kazul asked mildly.

"He'd better not," Cimorene said. "He's the one who was cheating, with the help of Zemenar and the rest of the wizards."

"Really," Kazul said in tones of great interest.

"It's all nonsense," Woraug declared. "The girl's just trying to attract attention."

"Really," Kazul said again, and smiled, displaying all her silver teeth.

"Oh, come now, Kazul. Surely you won't take a mere princess's word over mine," Woraug said.

"That depends entirely on what she says. Tell us about it, Princess," Kazul commanded.

So Cimorene told them. She brought the stone prince foward to explain what he had overheard the wizards and Woraug discussing in the banquet hall, and she made Alianora tell everyone about melting wizards with wash water and lemon juice. She told about getting to the Ford of Whispering Snakes on the first feather and being unable to convince any of the dragons to listen to her. She told about going to Morwen's house to find out where the wizards were, and about using the last feather to get to the wizards and melt them. She described Zemenar's unexpected appearance and subsequent melting, and the way Morwen had broken the wizards' spell, and she finished with an account of Woraug's futile attack.

"And then *he* landed" – Cimorene waved in the direction of the escort dragon – "and decided to bring us all back here. And I think somebody ought to go back to that clearing where the blackberries are before the next batch of wizards arrives. I don't know what they'll do when they find out what's happened, but . . ."

"Yes, I see," said Kazul. She turned to a pale green dragon beside her. "Take five or six of the younger dragons – the ones who've been talking about starting a wizard-hunt – and go have a look at this blackberry clearing."

"Yes, Your Majesty," said the pale dragon with a fierce grin.

"Surely you don't believe this!" Woraug said.

Kazul stared at Woraug without saying anything, and the dragons around the edge of the circle rattled their scales.

"Ah – Your Majesty," Woraug added hastily.

"Why should I disbelieve it?" Kazul said, still watching Woraug.

"The whole thing is preposterous!" Woraug said. "How could wizards do anything to affect Colin's Stone? Your Majesty."

Kazul looked at Cimorene.

"I'm sorry, Kazul," Cimorene said, shaking

her head. "I know *what* the wizards were trying to do, but I don't have the slightest idea *how* they were doing it."

"I believe I can explain that, Your Majesty," Morwen said. She stepped forward, tossing and catching the wizards' black rock casually in her right hand. "They were using this. I believe you'll find that it comes from the Caves of Fire and Night. From the King's Cave, in fact, where Colin's Stone was found. And one of the properties of the Caves of Fire and Night is that you can use one piece to cast spells which affect similar pieces."

"Just the way that impossible book says!" Cimorene exclaimed.

"DeMontmorency? Yes, I suppose he is fairly impossible," Morwen said.

"Is this sufficiently similar to Colin's Stone that the wizards could have affected the stone through it?" Kazul asked.

"Certainly, Your Majesty," Morwen said.

"This is—" Woraug began.

"—ridiculous, impossible, and unbelievable," Kazul said. "You've said that already. But I haven't heard you say anything particularly convincing in support of that attitude."

"Oh, really, Your Majesty!" Woraug said. "Next you'll be saying I poisoned King Tokoz!"

"It doesn't seem likely," Kazul admitted,

"since Tokoz was poisoned with dragonsbane, and dragons can't get anywhere near the stuff without feeling the effects."

"What if Zemenar made a . . . a dragonsbane-proof packet for him to carry it in?" Cimorene said, thinking of the bag Antorell had been carrying when she and Alianora met him in the valley. "Something that would melt when he dropped it in the King's coffee."

"I suppose it's possible," Kazul said. "But there's no evidence at all that Zemenar did any such thing."

"What would it have looked like?" Alianora asked suddenly. "Would it have been something like a very large tea bag?"

Everyone turned to look at Alianora. "I think that would have worked quite well, Princess," Kazul said. "Why do you ask?"

"Because Woraug had something like that with him when he went to see King Tokoz the night before the King was killed," Alianora said. "I saw it."

An angry muttering ran through the crowd of dragons.

"Lies!" Woraug snarled. "They're all lies!"

"Are they?" Kazul said coldly. "I don't think so. You must have wanted to be King very badly indeed."

"I—" Woraug darted a glance around the

circle of dragons. What he saw did not appear to reassure him. "No!"

"Consorting with wizards, killing the King, and plotting to cheat in the trials with Colin's Stone," Kazul said as if Woraug had not spoken. "Hardly proper behavior for a dragon."

The crowd muttered agreement. Cimorene looked from Woraug to Kazul and back. Woraug appeared to be terrified of something, but Cimorene could not tell what it was. He crouched and seemed to shrink away from Kazul, drawing in his wings in close and making himself as small as possible. Cimorene blinked. It was remarkable how much smaller Woraug could make himself look. In fact . . .

"He's *shrinking!*" Cimorene exclaimed.

"No!" Woraug cried again, but it was much too late. He shrank faster and faster, his wings melting into ridges along his back and his claws retracting. He was barely as tall as Cimorene's shoulder. Then, with a sudden shiver, he collapsed in on himself. A small rain of scales pattered to the ground. A moment later, an extremely warty toad with angry red eyes crawled clumsily out of the center of the pile.

"Is that – is that Woraug?" Alianora asked in a hushed tone.

The toad turned and glared at her, and she

stepped back a pace. The stone prince put a protective arm around Alianora's shoulders and glared back at the toad.

"Behave, or I'll step on you," he said.

"Yes, it's Woraug," Kazul said. She sounded almost sad. "That's what happens when a dragon stops acting like a dragon."

The toad turned his glare in Kazul's direction, then hopped off and disappeared among the stones along the riverbank.

Alianora shuddered. Kazul studied her for a moment. "You were Woraug's princess, weren't you? I'm sorry about all this, but it couldn't be helped. It won't take long to find you another dragon."

"I don't think you have to worry about finding her another dragon," Cimorene said. She had been watching Alianora and the stone prince, and an idea had occurred to her.

"What? Why not?" said Kazul.

"Because the stone prince fought with Woraug, and Woraug certainly didn't win. Doesn't that mean that he gets to rescue Woraug's princess?"

"I'm not sure the rules cover this situation at all," Kazul said. "But it sounds reasonable enough, and under the circumstances I doubt that anyone will object. Unless of course she does."

"Oh!" said Alianora, and blushed a rosy red. "No, I don't object at all!"

"Are you sure?" the stone prince said anxiously. "You won't mind waiting a while to marry me? I mean, if you're willing to marry me? You needn't, you know, if the idea doesn't appeal to you."

"It appeals to me very much," Alianora said, blushing redder than ever. "But why do you say that we have to wait?"

The stone prince sighed. "I still have to find a king and do him a great service, and that's bound to take a while."

"For a young man as intelligent as you seem to be, you're remarkably foolish," Morwen commented. "What on earth do you think you've just done?"

An expression of astonishment spread across the prince's face. "You mean the king I was supposed to service is the King of the *Dragons*?"

"Exactly," Morwen said. "And I doubt that you could do her a greater service than saving the throne from Woraug's plotting."

"That's settled, then," Kazul said. "Let's get the rest of the ceremonies finished and get back to the mountains. There's a great deal of work to be done."

The dragons all bowed, and eddies of movement began in various sections of the crowd.

Shortly, two dragons came forward carrying Colin's Stone. It looked like a long black log about three times as thick as Cimorene's waist and twice as tall as she was. The dragons laid it in front of Kazul and backed away. Another dragon appeared, holding a large circlet made of iron, with six spikes poking upward at intervals around the rim. Kazul set her front feet on the black stone, and the dragon set the circlet on her head. The crowd of dragons began cheering again, and after a few minutes they began forming a line to congratulate their new King and present their coronation gifts. Other dragons set up large tubs of wine and platters of meat and cheese, which were quickly surrounded.

In the middle of the presentations, the dragons Kazul had sent off to the blackberry clearing returned, and Kazul took a short break from accepting congratulations to hear what they had to say.

"The wizards showed up before we'd been there more than ten minutes, Your Majesty," said the pale green dragon who was the leader of the group. "Six of them, just like your princess said."

"They weren't happy to see us," the youngest dragon said smugly.

"I would think not." Kazul smiled. "What did you do with them?"

"We chased five of them away," the pale dragon reported. "I don't think they'll be back, either."

"Five?"

The pale dragon shot a glance at the youngest of the group, who licked his lips and looked even more smug than before and said nothing. "Yes, Your Majesty."

"I see. Well, that's more than enough evidence to confirm what Cimorene's told us," Kazul commented. She raised her voice. "The arrangement between the dragons and the Society of Wizards is hereby canceled. From now on, wizards will not be allowed anywhere near the Caves of Fire and Night, no matter what they say." Then she went back to accepting presents and congratulations from her new subjects.

Cimorene watched the festivities with mixed feelings. She was very glad that Kazul was the new King of the Dragons, but she couldn't help wondering what effect Kazul's coronation would have on her own position. The King of the Dragons certainly wouldn't need a princess as a mark of status and there would be plenty of younger dragons eager to cook and clean for their King, if only as a way of getting a start at the court.

Her preoccupation stayed with her for the rest of the day, through the entire coronation picnic and the flight back to the Mountains of Morning. Cimorene and Alianora rode on the back of a very large dragon whose scales were such a dark green that they looked almost black. Alianora would have preferred to ride with the stone prince, but none of the dragons were willing to take on a second passenger if the stone prince was the first. All of the dragons had paid their respects to Kazul at the coronation, so the cave was empty when the dragon dropped Cimorene off. When Cimorene said good-bye to Alianora, she promised to come over and help her pack the following morning. Then she went in and waited for Kazul to come home.

Kazul did not arrive until very late. She was still wearing the iron crown, and she looked very tired.

"Thank goodness that's over," she said, taking the crown off and throwing it across the cave. It hit the wall and bounced off with a harsh clang.

"You shouldn't treat your crown like that, Your Majesty," Cimorene said, retrieving the iron circlet.

"Of course I should," Kazul said. "It's expected. That's why we made it out of iron instead of something soft and bendable. And don't start calling me 'Your Majesty.' I've had enough of that for one day."

Cimorene began to feel a little better. "What happens next?"

"Tomorrow we start moving," Kazul said and sighed. "It will probably take weeks. It's too bad there's no way of warning a new king in time to pack everything up before the work starts."

"Everything?" Cimorene said in tones of dismay. "Even the library and the treasure vaults? But I've only just got them organized!"

"Everything," Kazul said. "And if you think straightening out things here was difficult, wait until you see the mess the official vaults are in."

"Oh, dear," said Cimorene. "Is it very bad?"

Kazul nodded. "I've just come from looking at it. You'll see for yourself tomorrow. There's a smallish cave next to the library that I think will do nicely for you, but I'd like you to look at it before we start hauling things around."

"You mean you want me to stay?" Cimorene blurted. "But I thought the King of the Dragons didn't need a princess!"

"Don't be ridiculous," Kazul said. "How am I going to get my cherries jubilee if you don't stay? And you haven't even started cataloguing the library, and how else am I going to get the King's treasure vaults arranged so I can find things? *I'm* not going to have time to do it."

"Won't the rest of the dragons object?"

Kazul snorted. "I'm the King. One of the advantages of being King is that nobody objects to whims like keeping a princess when you're not supposed to need one. If it bothers you, we'll give you a different title: King's Cook and Librarian, maybe. Stop worrying and go to sleep. Tomorrow is going to be a very busy day for both of us."

Cimorene smiled and went off to her rooms with a light heart. She slept soundly and was up early next morning. Kazul was already awake and supervising three of the younger dragons, who were packing up the treasure and the library. Since Cimorene was pressed into service at once, it was several hours before she could get away to keep her promise to Alianora.

"I'm sorry I'm late," Cimorene apologized when she arrived at Woraug's cave at last. "But it didn't occur to me that Kazul would be moving, too, and she wanted me to help."

"It's all right," Alianora assured her. "It wasn't as big a job as I'd expected, and the prince helped. I'm almost finished." She gestured at an almost-full suitcase lying open on the floor. On the other side of the room, the stone prince was stacking the empty drawers from Alianora's bureau.

"Well, at least I got here in time to say good-bye," Cimorene said.

"You're staying with the dragons, then?" the stone prince asked, straightening with a frown. "Are you sure you want to do that?"

"Of course she's sure," Alianora said. "Kazul's going to need her even more than she did before, and Cimorene wouldn't be happy in a normal kingdom."

"How did you know that?" Cimorene said, staring at Alianora.

"It's obvious. Linderwall is about as normal a kingdom as you can get. If you ran away from there, you certainly wouldn't be happy anywhere like it."

"I didn't mean that part," Cimorene said, reddening slightly. "I meant about Kazul wanting me to stay."

"That was obvious, too," Alianora said. "You're the only one who was worried about it." She studied Cimorene for a minute and shook her head. "I wouldn't like being princess for the King of the Dragons, but it will suit you down to the ground."

"I think it will," Cimorene said, smiling.

"Then maybe you can tell me something," the stone prince said. "What's being done about the wizards?"

"They've been banned from the Mountains

of Morning, and there are a hundred or so dragons out checking to make sure they've gone," Cimorene replied. "They haven't had much luck, I'm afraid. Most of the wizards left after the first few got eaten."

"That's all?" asked the prince.

"What else can the dragons do? The wizards didn't actually poison King Tokoz; Woraug did that. So there's no justification for an all-out attack on the headquarters of the Society of Wizards, even if all the dragons agreed that they wanted to do it. Which they don't."

"I suppose you're right," the prince said. "But you'd better tell Kazul to keep a close eye on them. Those wizards will make more trouble just as soon as they figure out a way to do it."

"I don't know about that," Cimorene said. "I think Zemenar was behind most of it, and you melted him."

"That's it!" Alianora said, and snapped her fingers. "I almost forgot to tell you. Morwen and I talked for a long time yesterday, and she says that melting a wizard isn't permanent."

"You mean they'll all come back?" Cimorene asked.

Alianora nodded. "It will take them a while, though. And Morwen said for you to come and visit soon. She thinks that in a few days she'll have figured out a way of melting wizards without dumping soapy water over them. 'A method that's a little less sloppy' was the way she put it."

"That will be useful if the wizards start making trouble again," Cimorene said thoughtfully.

"Is this everything, Alianora?" the stone prince asked, gesturing at the suitcase.

"Yes, I think so." Alianora pulled the top of the suitcase over, and the stone prince set one foot very gently in the middle of it and pushed until the latch clicked.

"Where are you going first?" Cimorene asked. "His kingdom or yours?"

"Neither," Alianora said, smiling. "We're going to Morwen's. She said she could change him back from stone to normal. We asked Kazul last night if we could go out through the Caves of Fire and Night, and she said yes, so . . ."

"I don't know, Alianora," the stone prince said. "I'm beginning to get used to myself this way. And there are certain advantages."

"There are disadvantages, too," Alianora said, blushing slightly.

Cimorene began to giggle.

Alianora's blush deepened. "I mean – uh – how are you going to get rid of that chip in your sleeve if you can't change clothes?"

"I think I see what you're getting at," the stone

prince replied, eyeing Alianora meditatively. "And you're quite right. There's no comparison. We had better see Morwen as quickly as possible."

Alianora and Cimorene looked at each other and burst into unstoppable giggles.

The stone prince blinked at them. "It's not funny!" he said indignantly, which only made them giggle harder. Shaking his head, he waited for them to stop, then picked up Alianora's suitcase. "Shall we go?"

Cimorene walked with them to the iron gate that led into the Caves of Fire and Night. A purplish dragon was waiting to guide them through the caves. Kazul was taking no chances on Alianora and the stone prince getting lost. Cimorene hugged them both and wished them a safe journey.

"And I hope you both live happily ever after!"

"I hope you do, too!" Alianora called back as she and the stone prince followed the dragon through the gate.

Cimorene watched until they were out of sight, then started back toward Kazul's cave. She thought about Morwen, and the wizard-melting spell, and about Zemenar and Antorell and the other wizards who would somehow be back soon. She thought about Kazul, and about straightening out the treasure vaults that belonged to the King of the Dragons, and about all the hundreds of books in the King's library, and of all the problems that the King of the Dragons would have to deal with. She thought about Alianora's last words and smiled.

Happily ever after? Cimorene wasn't sure about that, though she was certainly hoping to enjoy herself. She was positive, however, that life with the dragons would be interesting and busy, and in Cimorene's opinion that would go a long way toward making her happy.

"Happily ever after? I don't think it's quite what you meant, Alianora," Cimorene murmured to the empty tunnel, "but one way or another, I rather think I will."